I0555827

CUTHBERT
Home on the Range

#6

by

Patrick Barrett

A Wild Wolf Publication

Published by Wild Wolf Publishing in 2016
Copyright © 2016 Patrick Barrett

ISBN: 978-1-907954-55-9
Also available as an e-book

www.wildwolfpublishing.com

Chapter One

Elspeth finished stirring the mixture. She judged it ready by the 'click-click' of the wooden spoon against the sides of the old beige pottery mixing bowl. There wasn't a sound when the mixture was thick, but as it thinned out the magic sound appeared. *Huh,* she thought, *all these fancy cookery books and she had never once read about that.* She lifted the spoon slowly and tested the viscosity. Actually, she watched how fast it ran off, but you can't write a fancy cookery book telling them that.

Percy sat at the table, legs swinging with anticipation, his 'turned-down' wellies slapping gently.

Elspeth liked Percy, he was company. It was like borrowing someone's child, or a big dog. Enjoy the moment and as soon as it looked like making a mess, send it back. Elspeth smiled and began filling the little crinkled paper cases with mixture.

Percy's legs swung faster and he actually licked his lips. Elspeth had never had children, but somehow there had always been someone to 'lick the bowl out' and Percy was this year's contender.

With a breathless, "Thank you," he took the bowl, up-ended it and stuck his face in.

Elspeth sighed. *Men never grow up,* she thought. *They never let go of big cars, leather jackets or cake mix.*

Percy eventually lowered the bowl and handed it back. "Thanks, Elspeth," he said. "Perfect as always. You could win competitions for your cooking, you know."

Elspeth demurred gracefully as he confirmed her own beliefs.

Percy sat there grinning with a circle of cake mix around his face and into the fringes of his unruly red hair. The bowl had been licked clean, but it would still be wise to wash it thoroughly. Elspeth had seen where it had been!

The crow had waited patiently. Circling around the chimney, he had identified the baking smell on the up-draught. Now he settled on the rim and twisted around to warm his tail feathers. He had seen the 'Little scruffy one' enter the house and now all he had to do was wait.

Sure enough, the front door opened and closed and the two people made strange noises at one another.

3

The crow cocked his head to one side trying to use the other side of his brain. Birds only made a noise for a reason; they either wanted something, were about to announce something, or to pretend that someone else had whatever a bigger bird was looking for. That's why they were always nodding towards someone else's nest.

Humans seemed to make noises all the time, without any identifiable sequence. Meet someone (Babble), stand near someone (Babble) and walk away from someone (Babble).

And what is this obsession with doors? Surely if something is in the way every time you approach an opening, you will eventually be moved to take it off? Really!

Life was so simple up here; it was the humans who complicated things. Crows had shown them how to fly and what thanks did they get? Anything over five hundred feet high was sucked in, chewed up and spat out. Why couldn't they just flap their wings like everyone else?

The little scruffy one appeared, walking away from the house, and the crow poised himself. This was it, the rule of the predator. If it moves, eat it; if it turns out to be bigger than you, poke it in the eye and get the flap out of it. Of course, if it has already stopped moving, usually after head-butting a car, the same rules apply, but there's a bit more time to enjoy the result.

The crow launched itself and with one powerful flap watched its shadow fall across Percy. The scruffy little one wasn't the only one who liked cake mix!

Cuthbert didn't even jump as the door crashed open. Percy only had one way of entering a house. He looked around.

His friend had flattened himself against the wall and was gasping for breath. His hair was even more dishevelled than usual and threads stood up out of his hat. Amongst the scratches on Percy's face were little blobs of beige.

"Elspeth baking again?" asked Cuthbert.

4

Chapter Two

Elspeth and her husband, 'the Captain', entered the Mandrake Arms. Almost everyone was there and the evening was in full swing. Of course, 'full swing' was a relative term, the Valley had a rhythm of its own and it was barely discernible to outsiders.

Elspeth handed out little cakes and the women 'cooed' appreciatively.

The men carefully hid their relief at finding some palatable home baking and simply tucked in.

Accepting the thanks and praise generously, Elspeth prepared for the inevitable, and it wasn't long in coming.

"Of course," said the Captain, "I was quite a mean chef myself. Do you know what they called me in the regiment?"

Ronald mumbled, "Several things spring to mind, mate."

The Captain ploughed on regardless. "Still got my old field kitchen, you know, fantastic thing. Coffee bubbling in one compartment, horse-stew in another and bread baking on top. All pulled by stallions, environmentally friendly or what?"

Visions of a contraption with horses inside it and outside it seemed to take up most people's attention and of course, they all remembered this amazing vehicle from the Valley's golf match some time ago.

Margery finished one of Elspeth's cakes and dabbed her lips daintily. "You know, dear, you could win prizes with your baking."

Percy spoke up. "I said that too."

Elspeth blushed slightly and said, "Well, it's funny you should say that. There is a cookery contest touring the country and I wondered if the village should enter."

The men all nodded enthusiastically, but the women reacted rather strangely. They seemed to study one another carefully, as if to sniff out a rival rock cake at fifty paces. Each one had a speciality handed down by generations, some were even edible.

Gradually the women gathered in a corner and generally thrashed out who could contribute what and it was decided that a 'competition picnic' should be arranged and the men could act as the judges.

Arkle seemed distracted. "Did he say *horse*-stew?" she asked.

The men confirmed he had indeed said that, with only Henry

5

seeing the minefield ahead of them.

Margery separated herself from the group and addressed the men. "Of course, we are assuming that none of you will wish to enter, boys?"

Glances were exchanged around the table to a background of sniggering from the women. The Captain began to volunteer his wartime speciality, but caught Arkle watching him and sipped his drink instead.

Henry put up his hands in mock surrender and said, "I love food, but if I can't rip its lid off and microwave it, I'm lost."

The rest of them stared blankly. A Valley with no electricity didn't attract many microwave salesmen.

Ronald mentioned his jungle training and recommended a 'nice bit of squirrel'.

Percy's 'fry-ups' were legendary, but the presentation left a lot to be desired and Cuthbert thought that a 'poached egg' meant it had been stolen from the next farm. Glumly, they accepted their role of lesser mortals and left the women to it.

Suddenly Percy set down his drink and addressed the whole table. "Funny old thing, isn't it? All this fuss about food, one minute we're living in caves eating leaves and the next a woolly mammoth falls onto someone's fire and soon every weekend is barbecue time."

The Captain looked at him suspiciously. "Ancestor of yours was it?" he asked.

Ronald quipped, "Which, the mammoth?"

Percy rode the gales of laughter with ease. After everyone settled down, he continued, "No, really! Every day would have been taken up with finding food. If you didn't chase it, trap it or trick it, you couldn't eat it. That's why we have so much spare time now. Everybody knows where the supermarket is."

"You don't," mumbled Cuthbert.

Percy carried on, "Then suddenly, eating the stuff wasn't enough; it had to look right and it had to be expensive. A whole industry has grown up around something we used to do ourselves." Percy sat back.

"He's right, you know," said Henry. "I have sat in restaurants all over the world, where people would pay a fortune just to be seen there. The food really didn't matter; the point was that you could afford to be there. I suppose that means it has already evolved into an industry where even the food isn't necessary."

6

"Perhaps we should go back to being self-sufficient?" asked Ronald, already mentally tasting squirrel.

"Why? Are the women going somewhere?" asked the Captain in alarm.

The women were trying very hard to be civilised, but this was cooking! Every time an ancestral cookbook was slapped down on the table, another one landed on top to 'trump' it. In the end an original Mrs Beeton's dropped by Arkle flattened the lot and she was the only one who could lift it.

Margery suggested perhaps they should recreate a 'period' meal from Mrs Beeton's time. This was accepted as truly original and Arkle was given the job of 'page turner'. The women all craned their necks for a better view as the colour plates appeared and Arkle read out the procedures with relish.

"Do *what* to the hare?" asked Belinda in disbelief.

"They mean a real creature?" asked Avril, blanching.

"Chickens don't look like that nowadays," pointed out Geraldine.

Arkle slammed the book closed in despair. "Chickens aren't born wrapped in cellophane with their legs trussed, you ninny," she said. "Wait until you have to wrestle a pig to the ground and convince it to give up its bacon."

Lots of noses suddenly required powdering and Arkle was left to consider the fate of the great British farmer's wife. *A lost woman filled with lost arts in a lost world,* she thought shaking her head sadly. Hefting the book quite easily, she replaced it on the shelf, leaving a colourful pamphlet in top place. 'Big jellies for little bellies,' it announced cheerfully.

Percy was in an enquiring mood. "Why did the women assume that we can't cook?" he asked.

Cuthbert looked up from his crossword, pretending to be annoyed at being interrupted "Because we can't!" he snapped.

Surely seven down can't be radish? he thought. *One across seemed to be potato, but that would make fourteen down asparagus! Why were all the answers vegetables?*

He scowled at Percy. "Have you swapped your crossword for mine again?" he asked suspiciously.

Percy shrugged and ignored him. "We can cook; it just doesn't look as if it's been cooked when we slap it onto a plate."

7

Often Percy spent an hour in the doctor's surgery catching up on all the news in the out-of-date magazines. Last week, he was almost flying on his way home in a panic because the Japanese had attacked Pearl Harbour. Henry had given him a drink to settle his nerves and reminded him that the old doctor hadn't been outside for forty years, so everything was likely to be old news.

Now Percy removed a magazine from his inside pocket and flipped through it.

Cuthbert stared at his old friend. "Have you stolen that from the surgery?"

Percy glanced over the top and replied, "No, I took it without permission."

"Yes, Percy," said Cuthbert. "That's the definition of stealing."

"No, it isn't," sniffed Percy. "I'm very popular in these parts and anyone would have let me take it. But, there was nobody there to ask, so, if I couldn't ask permission, then it couldn't be granted. Therefore, I took it pending the permission, which would surely have been available, had there been someone in attendance."

Cuthbert asked as Percy paused to catch his breath, "So it was someone else's fault then?"

Percy grinned. "Precisely! Now, do you want to read this recipe or not?"

Cuthbert read slowly to try and counter Percy's enthusiasm. Nothing good ever came of Percy rushing. Come to think of it, nothing good ever came of Percy doing anything at any speed. "Set the oven to the desired temperature and bring a pan of water to the boil."

The saucepans were suspended from hooks above the cooking range and Percy made a grab for one, but only succeeded in swinging it to and fro like a ghoulish pendulum.

Cuthbert lifted them both down and read, "Put a measured amount of water into the saucepan." Hearing the rush of water, Cuthbert looked up in time to see Percy holding a turned down boot over the saucepan.

"There you go," said Percy proudly, "one welly full."

Cuthbert read on. "Apparently we need beeswax. Do you think they mean honey?" He looked at Percy "Have you got hives?"

Percy shook his head and suggested, "No, but the Captain has that rash on his leg."

Cuthbert continued to read as Percy rummaged in the cupboards.

8

The inside of a tin of furniture polish was added to the boiling pot. Cuthbert approached the cooking range. It had sat quietly building up a head of steam in the corner and little wisps of smoke were puffing out from under the door.

"This is my territory," he announced. "Stand back, Percy." He opened the door and his trousers turned to ash around his ankles as a gout of flame shot across the floor. Cuthbert glared at Percy. "Go on then. Say something to embarrass me," he challenged.

"Morning, Margery," said Percy, rising to the occasion.

"Morning, boys!" said Margery, cheerfully coming out of the lounge. She picked up the magazine and scanned the article. "Oh, good idea, boys," she said. "You'll enjoy making candles." As she left by the front door, she added, "Put some trousers on, Cuthbert. You never know who might drop by."

Cuthbert ran upstairs and found some smart trousers. He didn't have any smart legs to put them on, but he was in a hurry. Back downstairs he started tapping on panelled walls and listening for echoes.

Percy, with his unerring instinct for the blindingly obvious, asked, "Watch 'a doin'?"

Cuthbert tapped away and asked through gritted teeth, "How does she do it? How does she know her way around the secret tunnels like that?"

Percy sat to watch and put his feet up on an old elephant's foot umbrella stand. Yawning, he remarked, "I don't know why you insist on calling them 'secret tunnels'. Everyone knows about them."

"No, they don't," said Cuthbert, still tapping away.

"Yes they do," insisted Percy. "Only yesterday Elspeth was complaining about the one full of cobwebs."

Cuthbert stopped tapping and stared. "Which one is that?" he demanded.

Percy grinned. "Oh, that one *is* secret" he smirked.

Cuthbert glared at Percy and kicked the wall panel in frustration. The bang was repeated from within! Cuthbert stared and Percy stopped smirking. Cuthbert tapped twice. The two taps came back to him through the wall.

"There is something in there!" whispered Cuthbert.

Percy hazarded, "Perhaps its Elspeth with a duster," but without much conviction.

Cuthbert banged hard, three times. The same amount boomed back at him.

Percy picked out a solid walking stick and they stood each side of the panelled section. The wall swung inwards. Cuthbert gasped and Percy tensed.

The Captain entered and stumbled over the elephant's foot just as Percy swung the walking stick, missing the Captain and whistling over Henry's head as he came up some steps.

The Captain 'humphed' and said, "Haven't seen one of those since the colonial days; typical natives, give them an inch and they take a foot!"

The pair simply walked past and went into the kitchen, making all the sounds associated with putting the kettle on. Cuthbert peered into the doorway and across at Percy. They both shrugged and headed towards the kitchen.

Much to Cuthbert's annoyance, the newcomers agreed with Percy. "Oh yes, everybody knows about the tunnels now," they confirmed.

The Captain ventured, "You're an adventurous little chap, Percy. Haven't *you* explored them all?"

Percy looked cautiously at Cuthbert and replied, "Well, the gardening takes up most of my time, you know." Cuthbert gawped at him. They hadn't been separated by more than two feet for ages. Percy shuffled and continued, "You're right about the adventures though. One of my ancestors discovered the old world."

The Captain had to ask. "Don't you mean the *'New world'*?"

Percy elaborated. "Oh no, he left that to Columbus and Vasco Da Gama and that lot. Right publicity hungry bunch they were; he used to spend some time with a map maker and help out because he was so busy with all the explorers coming back and altering everything. Anyway, he noticed that while everyone was claiming the discovery of the new world, no-one actually claimed to have discovered the old one. So, he set off on a voyage up the Thames for a week or two, came back and had his name added to all the maps as having discovered the world they already lived in. It was seen as a bit of harmless fun until he sent a bill to Philip of Spain for rent. That's why the Spanish sent an Armada and my ancestor had to lie low for a while."

Henry simply carried on an earlier conversation with the Captain to numb his senses against Percy. "What happened to the other three feet then?" he asked.

The Captain pulled his thoughts together and said vaguely, "Oh, they put them behind the house and made a yard."

Each of them entered into a separate reverie until the door shook from someone pounding on the outside. "Come in?" ventured Cuthbert.

Arkle breezed in and dropped a huge block of something on the table. The table sagged as the ancient planks met their match, and dust pattered to the floor, "Heard you needed some inspiration chaps, so here it is," she boomed.

Percy prodded the lump with his finger and said, "So that's inspiration. No wonder new ideas are so hard."

Arkle put her hands on her hips and watched him very carefully. The Cuthbert one was bad enough, but this scruffy little one was a real horse-whip target. "Thought you could copy it and make some bread of your own to impress the women," she said, watching Percy like a hawk. "Or isn't it good enough?" she asked, voice dripping with menace.

As the recipient of the glare, Percy felt obligated to reply. Carelessly, he began, "No, no, it's fine, Ar …"

"Ar?" she asked.

"Aaarr," stumbled Percy, desperately looking to the others.

Arkle smiled like a killer stoat as she commented, "Nasty throat you've got there, Percy- like me to wrap something around it?"

Percy simply stared like a rabbit in the headlights until Arkle announced, "I'll leave it with you then," and left.

Exhaling, Percy said, "For Pete's sake, Henry, what *did* you name that daughter of yours?"

Henry looked bewildered. "Don't rightly know; I was abroad at the time."

A casual knock announced Ronald's arrival and he joined them in an inspection tour of Arkle's offering. "Is it a meteorite?" he asked.

It took the four of them to slide the block off the table. It crashed to the floor and stayed there like an extra chair.

"What do you think it really is?" asked Cuthbert.

"Kryptonite!" breathed Percy in awe.

"Don't be silly!" snapped Ronald and Henry was glad someone sensible had stepped in quickly. His shoulders slumped though, as his brother continued, "Kryptonite is green. Everyone knows that."

"Only inside," retorted Percy. "You have to check it with x-ray vision first. *Everyone* knows *that*."

11

"Gentlemen," tried Henry, "surely we are not going to have an argument about cartoon men in tights?" He looked around at the shocked expressions and sighed.

For a moment it looked as if the Captain would back him up, until he said, "Dashed unfair, Henry. Batman didn't wear tights, you know."

The argument raged. Percy was of the opinion that Superman could conquer all. Ronald pointed out that Batman didn't fall over every time someone pointed a rock at him. Percy retaliated with the fact that half the historic buildings wouldn't support 'somebody with pointy ears swinging off the gargoyles.'

The Captain tried to enter the 'Silver Surfer' as a candidate, but was met with derision from all sides. It was generally thought that 'a grown man wrapped in tinfoil without weapons would basically have travelled a very long way on a surfboard for very little result.'

Henry watched the passion of the debate. Fingers jabbed, lips curled and fictional facts flew like shrapnel. He felt a reassuring hand on his shoulder.

Margery had returned and hopefully brought some sanity with her.

Henry stood. *Time to end this all on a note of unstoppable reason,* he thought. "I have a question," he said. All eyes turned to him. "How would Batman claim tax relief on his costumes, cars, tyres and public liability insurance without giving away his secret identity?"

Confused silence resulted. Henry had stopped them in mid-flow.

Margery gripped his arm proudly as she said, "Anyway, Wonder Woman would have whipped the lot of them."

It all began again as Henry left, closing the door behind him.

Chapter Three

The idea of a national baking contest appealed to Marvin. He was always under pressure to promote the area using spare funds which would otherwise be subtracted from next year's budget.

The new cemetery and the memorial wall to fallen authority colleagues had rather surprisingly not attracted many visitors. This could be the answer. It could become an annual event like those book festivals where people were seen buying all the latest books before selling them on e-bay the next day.

Perhaps his wife could be offered a consultancy. 'Doreeen!' had become rather demanding again since the glare of publicity had died down and this would leave her less time to compile 'jobs-lists' for when he got home.

Marvin paused and savoured his moment. This was a local authority epiphany. They could enter the contest themselves with locally named treats! Everyone had heard of the Bakewell Tart and the Eccles Cake. Perhaps the time had come for the Valley. He doodled with complimentary names involving the local authority, 'Coconut Council Fancies' came to mind, as did 'Council Custard Cream Cakes'. He had to keep scrubbing out 'Marvin-Burgers' and 'Doreeen Dainties', because he was very aware that ambition had to be wrapped in secrecy, not just in pastry.

The road gang had been moved into new accommodation. They stood together in the centre of the room and looked around uneasily. It was clean, airy and had all the facilities, but it just didn't smell right.

As the leader, the drains inspector began with, "Well, this is nice lads, we'll soon settle in."

One lung Louie tried, "Hurr, hurr, I can't breathe with all these windows open."

Swivelling Simon forced his good eye to track steadily around and said, "It's so big I can't see everything at once!"

Buster was impressed. The foot scraper at the door had alerted him to a sense of change and he looked around in wonder.

Louie had wandered off into another room and he ran back in a

13

panic. "Hurr, hurr, hurr," he stammered as he caught his breath. "Place is jerry-built. There's a leaking pipe in there, I'm soaked."

The drains inspector dashed to the site of the emergency, but came back looking sheepish. "That's a shower, Louie," he said.

The women were finding that co-operation wasn't as easy as they had imagined. None of the women seemed capable of understanding that one woman's scone was another woman's declaration of war.

Diplomatic language was pure phonetics compared to the flowery rejections being invented here. "Oh, but my dear, I'm sure that your creation would be wasted upon the unsophisticated palettes around here."

Or, "Oh yes, dear, I saw someone try that once, but it wasn't a success," accompanied by a hand-rocking motion that suggested half the population of a large city had ceased to exist.

Margery sighed and decided the only way forward was to establish each woman's speciality and allocate it to her. That way each of them could contribute and share the glory. There might even still be someone left alive at the end to compete.

The road gang were settling in. Every movement was punctuated by, "Oops, sorry," followed by frantic rubbing sounds. Every time they moved or touched something, it left a mark or a smudge or a footprint on the pristine surfaces. Even simply moving about caused bits to drop off them! The strain was terrible; they hadn't even boiled the kettle yet. The drains inspector knew this was bad for morale and sat to analyse the situation. Then he stood guiltily, put some paper on his chair and tried again.

Today's discussion around Cuthbert's kitchen table was 'Town versus Country'. Ronald was a city boy. He'd seen enough jungles, swamps, deserts and fields to last him a lifetime.

Henry had been a staunch townie but somehow the Valley had 'got to him,' and now he was a passionate convert.

The Captain had also spent many years in far flung countries where strangers were trying to kill him. An ironic thought crossed his mind. Several times it may have been Ronald!

Cuthbert was Valley born and bred. He could only listen to everyone else's adventures and realise he had saved himself a lot of bother.

Percy had certainly been around. According to Ronald, only 'horse muck' could be spread over a wider area than Percy, and at least it carried benefits.

Jasper was a surprising contributor; he seemed to have an incredibly wide-ranging knowledge. When questioned, he attributed it all to 'Google'. The others nodded wisely, but all the Valley mafia had strange names and no-one was sure which one was Google.

Ronald made the point that whilst there was always a 'Village idiot', there was no such thing as a 'City Idiot'. This clearly elevated city dwellers above the country cousins.

Jasper contributed, "What about the 'City that never sleeps?' That sounds pretty dumb."

Percy leaned across the table and stabbed his finger at Ronald. "I know for a fact that city dwellers are only allowed to advance so far, and no further. I've seen the signs."

"What signs?" asked Ronald curiously.

Percy sat back and stated smugly, "City Limits."

Jasper joined him with, "If they don't comply, they can be shot with the city ordnance."

Percy came in with, "A village can be left unlocked all night too. Your lot need a key to the city."

"Anyway," said Jasper, "Not every village has an idiot."

Eyes slid furtively sideways and lips compressed. "Pardon?" asked Cuthbert.

The drains inspector had concluded that the problem was not actually with the road gang, it was with the perception of the road gang.

Amongst the hierarchy of the Local Authority, there seemed to be a conception that the road gang stank. This attitude was causing psychological ripples and affected his men's self-esteem.

No-one ever came near them in the old cabin, so the rumours were never confirmed. Therefore, if people could be kept away until the new building had acquired its identity, his men could concentrate on the arterial sewage systems without constantly stopping to think about

15

(Shudder) hygiene.

To this end, the drains inspector fastened a plaque to the door stating clearly, 'Danger-Radioactivity - Do not enter'. It had worked a treat. No-one came around to borrow sugar or leave memos or anything. Of course, he had to take it down again to entice the road gang to enter, but he was sure they would get the idea eventually.

The women had a problem and it was to do with shape. Not the shape of the women, they covered every geometric parameter between them. It was the shape of the bread. Each of them would submit a loaf of a certain type and in an individual shape.

Arkle claimed to have already done one, but Margery convinced her to 'try something smaller this time, dear.'

The problem was that the amount of yeast needed for them all to submit an offering was far too big for any of their ovens, but it had to all be ready together, so that one person could enter the bread for the final.

After calculating the amount and allowing Arkle to pummel it into submission, the women were forced into a reluctant conclusion. Only Cuthbert had an oven big enough.

Cuthbert's kitchen was a hive of activity when Margery, Avril and Arkle arrived. Percy had taken his wellies off and was banging them on the table. They weren't a great fit at the moment, either something was stuck in the toes or his toe-nails needed cutting. Cuthbert had been 'servicing 'the hand pump over the sink. He shoved his hand up the spout and wriggled it about. Then he struck it with the hammer he used to knock burnt-bits off the cooking range and finally he had pleaded with it.

The women entered when Cuthbert opened the door and Margery stared at Percy who had disappeared up to his shoulder in his own welly. She focused on Cuthbert with a hammer in his hand, grinning inanely. Cuthbert thought she was disorientated by actually entering through the door for once.

Easing Arkle in front, Margery explained what the women needed his cooking range for, and Arkle dropped a huge lump of dough on the table. "We will go and get the rest of the contestants and our bread moulds and we will be back soon, Cuthbert. Be a dear and don't eat it up," she joked.

16

Cuthbert and Percy surrounded the lump and watched it from several angles. It didn't move.

Percy lifted one corner and showed Cuthbert the perfect impression of the wooden planks moulded into it. "Why did she say *don't* heat it up?" asked Percy. "It won't be ready for when they get back."

Cuthbert pondered, "I thought she said 'you won't heat it up.' She probably doesn't realise how hot this range can get. Right, we'd better get this cooked, or it will be our fault again. They only include us so there is someone to blame."

Percy agreed and they lifted one end each, but the middle flopped down between them. By laying planks from the table top to the oven door it became easier to roll the whole thing into place. "That's using your loaf, Cuthbert," quipped Percy.

The lump was gradually pushed and squeezed into the largest oven and the door fastened shut with its locking bar. The two friends sat back and savoured the rich aroma of baking bread and the sound of creaking metal.

Almost skipping along the farm track, the women thought there was something so traditional about all this. Wicker baskets over their arms, clean cloths to cover the bread, and bread moulds taken from above the ingle-nook, well, pantry cupboard in most cases.

"You know," said Margery, "I can almost smell baking bread already."

"Good Lord, so can I," said Elspeth.

Avril, slightly ahead, turned and asked, "You know those old stories about a gingerbread house in the woods?"

"Ooh yes, we could make one of those," trilled Elspeth.

Avril shook her head to clear her vision. "I think Cuthbert already has."

The beige mixture had oozed out of the windows lifting the thatched eyebrows in surprise. As the women watched, a huge bubble came out of the chimney and gave a loud 'pop!' The next bubble formed just as the crow landed on the edge of the chimney pot to investigate the wonderful smell. Suddenly he was enveloped inside a warm sphere and rising away from the troubles of the world. He had an awful suspicion he was heading for the troubles of the next one though.

Cuthbert and Percy clunked around the corner of the farmhouse.

Each of them had a lump of baked bread for hands, and large

17

round beige feet. Hats of 'crusty white' perched above them and they grinned triumphantly. "It's all right, ladies," called Percy, "we are safe!"

"Oh no, you're not," muttered the women as they ran forward swinging their bread moulds.

Percy and Cuthbert had a goat each. They also had a length of rope each. This would imply they were in charge of the goats, but no-one is ever in charge of a goat. Having run all the way into the next valley, the pair sheltered in a haystack and had woken up as the goats introduced themselves. As introductions go, having one's hands and feet eaten by creatures with vertical irises and cloven hooves, comes close to shaking hands with a crocodile.

Once most of the bread had been eaten, leaving them quite a bit lighter, Percy and Cuthbert found the goats' owner and arranged to borrow them.

The journey home was a tedious affair. Every thistle, every flower head and every discarded sock had to be investigated, tasted and shared.

Percy became really fed up and put his goat into a discarded supermarket trolley. Charging up behind Cuthbert and coming out of the morning mist, he looked like a Viking long-ship on a raiding holiday.

Eventually, the friends returned to the Valley. Percy and his goat had swapped places now and again with Percy in the wire trolley pulling faces and the goat butting it along from behind.

Standing at the farmhouse door and staring at the volcanic ooze hanging out of all the openings, the goats couldn't decide whether this was heaven or hell, but they started tucking in anyway.

With any luck, thought Cuthbert, *they will soon eat enough space out to be able to put the kettle on.*

Meanwhile, they needed somewhere to stay. Percy was appalled. "My place," he ranted, "why my place?"

"Because it's all we've got," pointed out Cuthbert. "Anyway, you've been living at my place for long enough, haven't you?"

"Seems like long enough," muttered Percy.

Percy's shed was exactly as he had left it. The three legged armchair with the plant pot under it and the shelves groaning with 'gardening' trophies. It was obvious to anyone that the trophies were sports ones from charity shops and Percy had broken off a vital piece from each of them. He claimed that the darts player was picking apples. The man bowling was checking his strawberries and the painful looking Karate kick was a rain dance.

He begrudgingly made room for Cuthbert amongst a pile of magazines.

Cuthbert leafed through one of them and was relieved to read that the war was over at last.

Percy clumped about muttering about 'his bachelor pad' and 'security' for his trophies.

The rain began a mischievous pattering on the roof and soon came inside to join them.

Marvin was elated. He knew a winner when he saw it and he also recognised the sound of opportunity. On top of that, he could smell success and taste victory. All in all, he was in sensory heaven.

The mayor had been won over immediately. Visions of annual cake contests bringing in revenue and celebrity chefs visiting, had caused him to wax lyrical, but as a man of limited polish or lyrics, he rather disappointingly came up with, "This could put us on the map."

Marvin had ventured into 'cubicle city' and mentioned the plan to the female staff. They had 'oohed' and 'aahed' in all the right places, but the passion wasn't there. When he had asked for each of their 'specialities', he was offered 'Copying', typing' and ham sandwiches.

The cleaning lady clonked her disapproval against the galvanised bucket, until he asked her opinion. "Well, if you want my opinion," she offered modestly, "this bunch has only ever cooked their own goose."

Marvin saw what she meant. All mid-day snacks came in plastic tubs or shrink-wrapped anti-theft covering.

He went home that evening with a heavy heart. He had only one course left open to him. He would have to consult 'Doreeen!'

'Doreeen' was painting her nails. He shuddered, he had forgotten about her nails. He tried very hard to forget about her, but marriage was an extension of the soul with a cold grip upon the heart.

She concentrated upon the flick of the little brush and the depth of the sheen until Marvin mentioned 'celebrity chefs.'

Doreeen was all nails and ears now. Waving imperiously for

19

silence, Marvin's wife began to speak. The combination of nails on blackboards and gravel beaches at high tide combined to make Marvin cringe and his fists to clench. "I will need *people!*" she shrilled.

Now *people*, Marvin understood, were a strange breed that stayed in the shadows and only appeared when 'Doreeen' needed help. *They may as well live in the attic*, thought Marvin. *It would be cheaper to adopt them.*

Chapter Four

Cuthbert tossed and turned, Percy snored. Cuthbert kicked him, Percy still snored. Cuthbert gave up and wandered outside.

It was a beautiful night spattered with stars. It was as if someone had put a lid on the Valley. Cuthbert had seen lots of changes in the Valley lately, but still knew every inch of the ground; every tree, every wall and every *strange red glow in the distance*?

Cuthbert looked around, he was disorientated. He studied the stars to get his bearings, but gave up and followed the path instead. The glow was flickering- someone had a fire and he could hear chanting. Cuthbert had belly-crawled around these parts as a young lad and could creep up silently and unseen. He topped a small rise and looked down at the scene below.

The Valley mafia sat in a circle around a fire and Jasper read from an old book. The others were repeating phrases and chanting them back at him.

Cuthbert stared- witchcraft in the Valley? Then another thought struck him. Perhaps this is where Jasper consulted Google? Some strange, all knowing God left over from the primeval beliefs of the past. Cuthbert edged closer using all his skills to stay invisible until he was in the slightly deeper shadow of a bush.

"Good evening," said a pleasant voice in his left ear.

Cuthbert ran.

Percy was being shaken, he knew that. His eyes were rolling, his lips were totally unsynchronised and his hat was over his eyes. Percy sat up sharply and tried to focus as his features rearranged themselves.

Cuthbert was flat against the wall now making frantic hand signals the way Ronald did when he forgot the right ones and made them up. "Oh, for goodness sake, have the pile of magazines, Cuthbert. I'll have the chair," he yawned.

Cuthbert was still signalling frantically; holding a finger over his lips and making cutting strokes across his throat at the same time.

Percy assumed he had swallowed a large melon and wanted someone to cut his head off to retrieve it. *Funny how the mind works when you've just woken up*, he thought. He crawled over to his friend and Cuthbert whispered urgently, "Valley mafia, black mass, fire, summoning the great God Google."

After another yawn, Percy replied, "No, they're not. Jasper's mum is redecorating and they meet out here until the paint's dry."

"But, but," stammered Cuthbert, "old book of spells, chanting!"

"Recipes," said Jasper from the other side of the door. "We have to chant out the ingredients 'cos not many of us can write."

Cuthbert opened the door. "Why are you chanting ingredients?" he asked, trying to show a grain of reason in his desert of panic.

Jasper shrugged. "Just normal juvenile curiosity," he said, "Once we have worked out how much everything costs, we can stock-pile supplies and corner the market; that way, you lot will have to come to us for everything you need for the competition."

Percy pointed out, "You may just be out of luck, you know, lads."

"Why?" Jasper asked suspiciously.

"They may send Arkle to do the shopping," he said with a grin.

Cuthbert and Percy tried to settle down again, but it was impossible.

They both sat up and Percy asked, "Did I ever tell you about that relative of mine who pioneered a method of preserving cultures and was responsible for curing millions of people?"

"No, you didn't," said Cuthbert, unable to fight his way to the door.

"Well," Percy shuffled.

Cuthbert groaned.

"Stuck in traffic one day, it was noticed that the pattern of mud splashed on the back of the van in front, made exactly the same shaped group as the virus pattern they were working on at the lab. Back at the lab, a team was assembled to investigate and find a method to replicate the shape. They tried all sorts of ways. Flinging mud at random, spinning it in a centrifuge and even flicking it from their fingers. Eventually, they made the same shape as another virus, which meant that the antidote could be spread exactly over the virus and kill it. It worked! It was just a case now of matching as many shapes as possible to kill all the deadly viruses."

Cuthbert had no choice but to be impressed. "So did your relative discover the pattern?"

22

"Oh no, that was another chap," said Percy hesitantly.

Cuthbert tried again. "So he discovered the method then?"

"Er, no, that was someone else too," admitted Percy uncomfortably.

"So what did he do then?" demanded Cuthbert.

"He drove the scientist who spotted the mud in the traffic jam," he admitted sheepishly.

Chapter Five

The next morning found them outside Cuthbert's farmhouse. There was one goat-shaped hole where the door used to be and it split into two goat-shaped tunnels leading inside where they had separated.

Percy seemed to be the right shape, so he was sent in to investigate. A small crowd gathered, hoping for some drama, and they were rewarded when Percy's wellies were butted out without him.

Eventually, Percy reappeared covered in crumbs like a 'cookie-monster'. Brushing himself down, he revealed that the goats had gone their separate ways. One had gone uphill and was in the attic and the other one was in the cellar. The kettle was still hidden like a relic in a lost tomb.

The crow wasn't exactly up on new inventions, but he knew that the skies were pretty crowded these days.

He had seen the high flyers leave a long white rip in the sky and he had heard the little whiney ones lower down.

The one that all crows tried to avoid was the one with a spinning disc on top. What on earth an egg whisk was doing up here was beyond him, but this one really burst his bubble.

The road gang were adopting strategies now. If someone bumped against the wall, it was pointless taking hours scrubbing at the spot and then having to repaint; it was much quicker to put a training poster over it.

The drains inspector was delighted with this one. It gave the appearance of an office of professionals. That was another thing. The last place had been a cabin. This was an *office*!

They began to meet 'back at the *office*!' Sometimes they were late for the *office*! The drains inspector's favourite was when he was out and there was a problem, he would contact someone '*back at the office*!' In fact, he began to realise that he needed to carry several forms and safety leaflets around with him. He really could do with something to put them in when he '*left the office*!'

24

The drains inspector was slightly late the next morning and the road gang were having tea when he arrived.

Simon's eye began to swivel outrageously as he spluttered, "Is that a *briefcase?*"

One lung Louie struggled with, "Hurr, hurr, have you got stripes down your leg?"

Buster glanced up and simply commented, "That new safety helmet's no good. There's nowhere to fix a lamp."

The drains inspector stood defiantly. "I happen to think that as your superior, it is beholden to me to represent the noble office of drains and ancillary tunnels specialists and to dress in the manner fitting for that *office*! I have been in contact with an official body and I am now the official representative of the **N**ational **U**nion for **M**ining and **B**oring - **N**ormally **U**nderground **T**unnelling **S**pecialists.

"NUMB-NUTS?" asked Simon incredulously.

The drains inspector carefully checked on his fingers and said reluctantly, "Er, yes."

Louie was so much beside himself that his voice came out in stereo, "Hurr, betrayed his class. That's what he's done, hurr."

Buster simply said, "You look like a flour-grader."

The strategy meeting in the Mandrake Arms was turning into humiliation for the men. They sat over their drinks as the women fell about laughing over suggestions to personalise the cooking entries.

Geraldine had started it. Margery suggested 'Cuthbert fancies' and Geraldine had shrieked "Cuthbert fancies Percy!"

This had led to 'Percy Plumm-Duff' followed by 'Cuthbert's in custard' topped off by 'Percy's pig-less pork pie'.

The rest of the men kept their heads down; when the women were this creative, everyone was at risk.

Percy glared and returned his own broadside. "Well, Belinda Truffle has no need to talk for a start," he began.

Margery wasn't too pleased to be christened 'Margarine.' Avril became avocado, Geraldine became gelatine and Elspeth was 'fairy cakes'. Actually she quite liked that. Arkle waited patiently whilst unscrewing a table leg, but for once wisdom overcame wit and Percy missed her out.

The meeting degenerated into a slanging match where the women were demoted from 'maids of honour' to 'iron maidens' and the women agreed that anything half-baked would simply be 'man'.

Marvin went looking for the drains inspector. Since the cabin had been taken from them, he hadn't really thought about the road gang.

After asking around, he had been directed to an office claiming to be radio-active. Giving a briefly managerial knock, he entered.

A man looking vaguely familiar stood to greet him. The drains inspector was immaculate in pinstripes and he had a bowler hat on his hat stand.

Marvin had nothing on his hat stand and this office was huge. He accepted the offer of a coffee and looked around.

Posters adorned the walls emblazoned with legends like 'Tunnel for victory.' 'Safety first, blockages second!' screamed another one.

Marvin could sense a rival. Years of climbing the cargo net of Local Authority promotion had sharpened his instincts and his will to cling on tight. He could also smell ambition, but unfortunately with the drains inspector's new incarnation, he couldn't smell anything at all. Marvin smiled and asked, "So, drains inspector, what are your plans for the future?"

The goats were being downright uncooperative. They obviously had too much of a good thing and were straying off in all directions.

When Percy next checked the tunnels, it was like an ants nest. He couldn't reach anywhere in the house where there was anything of any use.

The goats seemed to have an instinct for being useful and useless at the same time.

Molten bread mix oozing out from under the door showed that the cooking range was getting dangerously hot and needed rescuing.

The usual gang of village layabouts collected and offered comments.

The Captain asked if they had found the kettle.

Henry asked whether anyone had patented the term, 'Farmhouse loaf' yet.

Ronald just pointed out that the neighbourhood had improved since the goats moved in.

Jasper and his Valley mafia stood back and watched. There had to be a way to make money out of this. Suggestions about contacting the papers had been rejected. The media didn't enter the Valley unless accompanied by a U.N. patrol, and any mention of Cuthbert invoked the quarantine laws. He stood stroking his chin and vaguely felt a tug on his sleeve.

"Jathper," somebody said.

Jasper came out of his reverie and turned. He stood rigid as his eyes tried desperately to focus on any one thing at a time. His eyes and his brain were in combat.

It was a girl! It had freckles on its nose! It had pigtails! It was right in the middle of a secret Valley mafia meeting!

"Jathper," she said again, "we could make lot'th of little loaveth and thell them for dollyth picnicth!"

"Who are you?" gasped Jasper, needing to know who was responsible for this heresy.

The girl simpered and somehow swung her hips as she stood there. "I'm your couthin Pearl. Your Mum thaid you'd be up here."

Jasper now had a command decision to make. He must appear in control for the sake of his men and there was only one person to blame. "*Mum,*" he wailed.

Marvin watched the drains inspector carefully and the rest of the team pretended to be busy, but eyes were slit and sliding sideways like in an old fashioned western, where the music suddenly swelled and someone went for his gun.

"Why do you actually *need* an office drains inspector? I thought all those pipes were laid outside and underground."

The whole team gasped. This was a typical office-wallah's view of the world, where all things are made of paper and tea came from machines.

The drains inspector studied his superior and, holding his temper in check, pointed out, "A hole cannot be dug when the frost makes the ground too hard, nor can it be dug when things are too muddy." His gritted teeth ached.

"Can't dig in the rain either, it floods your boots and causes 'Trench foot,' it does, hurr," contributed Louie.

"Bright sunshine causes headaches and dazzles the man swinging

27

the pick too," said another team member.

"Of course, hurr, we can't even find the job if it's foggy," added Louie.

Marvin stared at each of them in turn. "So basically," he began, "you can't work if it's wet, dry, muddy, sunny or foggy- how about windy?"

The drains inspector sucked in his breath sharply and said, "Never! The wind blows the tent over and puts the fire out. We can't work without a cup of tea either, can we?"

The whole team nodded vigorously at this.

Marvin steepled his fingers and said quietly, "Oh, I see it now, gentlemen. You definitely need an office, but the question is; do you actually need a VAN?"

Chapter Six

Cuthbert and Percy resolved to start digging themselves. How hard could it be to burrow into a huge cottage loaf and find a kettle?

Ronald shook his head at the limited imagination of civilians. "Stand back, lesser mortals," he said. Extracting a cylinder from under his coat, he pulled out a pin and threw it into the tunnel nearest the kitchen. A low whoomf preceded a cloud of smoke and a brilliant flash of light from inside.

"Shouldn't we have established where the goats were first, Ronald?" asked Henry.

"Well, there's one," said Cuthbert, pointing to a horned head sticking out of the chimney.

Percy grabbed his pick-axe and entered the front door like a dwarf trying to escape Snow White's incessant tidying up. He gave the impression that the other six weren't far behind. Sounds of clunking and cursing followed and he came back out, throwing his bent pick to the floor. "Marvellous," he said, glaring at Ronald, "the extra heat has turned the kitchen into one big scone!" He stormed off muttering mysteriously, "I hate currants!"

The crow landed gently on the rim of the chimney pot and pretended to preen himself before noticing the goat glaring at him with those odd vertical irises.

Studying the situation, the crow thought, *Stuck are we? Big silly curved horns won't let you fall back down, eh?*

Cocking his head about far more than was necessary, he allowed the goat to think he was weighing all the options. The eyes followed every movement.

Remember all those times when somebody looking very much like you chased me away from some tasty road-kill aperitif?

It was difficult for a crow to lick his lips, but he got the message through.

Feet began to scrabble inside the chimney.

The crow slowly and carefully began to scrape his beak along one of the goat's horns. Back and forth (rasp), back and forth (rasp). *Need a sharp beak for this one,* he thought, *this meal is not going down anytime soon.*

29

The goat's feet found some purchase inside the chimney and he suddenly shot *upwards* to land on the thatch with a diabolic smile to match the eyes.

Oops, thought the crow, batting furiously at the air with wings he had left in neutral.

Marvin tapped his pencil against his desk. The staccato rattle of his drum solo echoed around his tiny office.

Here was a man born to face challenges. He had been forged in the brutal survivalist world of the Local Authority. He had beaten off challengers before and had relished the victories. Somehow though, as time went by, challenges not only threatened his arteries, they threatened his pension. There would be little point in being a past hero of the Local Authority struggle if someone took the gold-plated pension slot above him. Or, heaven forbid, he was bumped down a grade.

It was bad enough the taxpayer ensuring a worry free future for someone they had never met, it was his duty to make sure it was paid to someone who deserved it. There was only one name on *that* list.

The drains inspector led his men back to the office. Gallantly standing aside, he allowed them to go first, so that he could supervise them going through the routine of wiping their feet, washing their hands and covering all shiny surfaces.

Buster, Louie and Simon began gathering in corners and whispering.

The drains inspector made a note to look out for any literature from 'Red Ronnie.'

"Well, it worked when Percy dropped a bag of flour down the drains," insisted Cuthbert. He was trying to convince the others that putting the hosepipe down the chimney was a good idea.

No-one bothered to ask how Percy had happened to be carrying a bag of flour anywhere near to a drain, because it might involve a story, and headaches were hard to shift without a cup of tea.

Jasper was about to make a wonderful point about the effects of

30

hydraulics upon degradable objects in confined spaces, but someone was pulling on his sleeve again.

A voice began, "Jathper ..." but was mercifully drowned out by the reappearance of Percy on his tractor.

The noise vibrated the bones in the inner ear and convinced everyone that their teeth were chattering. Percy switched off the engine and grinned down at everyone. "Just been fitting the centrifuge we use for spraying manure right over the fields, this will shift it." With a glance at Ronald, he instructed, "Stand back, lesser mortals," and switched the engine on again.

Driving up to the front door, Percy aimed the nozzle into the goat tunnel and threw a lever. A loud 'whooshing' sound accompanied the engine racket.

The goat still on the roof felt the vibrations through all four hooves. The goat still inside felt the vibrations too, right up its backside as it was propelled through the tunnels at high speed and fired out of the chimney amidst a spray of fine brown droplets. Landing awkwardly in front of its mate, it skidded to a halt and two pairs of vertically-slit eyes focused on the scene below.

Percy switched the engine off and scratched his head. "Is that all that came out?" he asked.

Cuthbert sniffed the air. "Did you empty that thing before you used it?" he asked.

Ronald uncovered his ears and demanded, "Does it have to be that noisy?"

Henry looked concerned. "Are those goats coming for us?"

Jasper arrived home having leapt over stiles, crawled through culverts and swung from trees. He glowed from boyish activity and the thrill of evading two angry goats. All his men were accounted for and the secret handshake had been agreed ready for next week. What could possibly go wrong on a day like this?

"Where's Pearl?" asked his Mum.

The Valley mafia answered the alarm call and spread out to search for 'some girl whose got Jasper's goat' as the instruction now read.

When they found her, they didn't really know what to do with her. The pretty dress she had worn was now some sort of sludgy tie-dye. Her pig-tails stuck out like semaphore arms and her freckles had

31

disappeared under the mud. If she had been a 'he', they would have slapped her on the back, had a good laugh and given her a new nickname. But, faced with this sobbing wretch who walked like a robot, nothing really suggested itself.

One of the more ambitious members suggested they would need to elect a new leader after this one arrived home.

Chapter Seven

Cuthbert and Percy stood in the office of the drains inspector. Cuthbert was nervous and started pacing. Every time he moved, someone placed a sheet of newspaper under his feet, which made him even more nervous.

Percy hadn't realised what a posh outfit this was. Somehow he'd imagined them to be a right scruffy bunch.

The drains inspector steepled his fingers and studied Cuthbert. "Bread, you say, a house full of bread?"

Cuthbert nodded.

"With tunnels in it?" continued the inspector.

Cuthbert stopped pacing and nodded again.

The drains inspector sat back and puffed out his cheeks, "Well," he began, "we usually unblock things involving rather smelly items."

Cuthbert glared at Percy, "Don't worry," he said, "someone's taken care of that already."

The drains inspector stood and faced his team. "Men," he said, "fetch the van, the community needs us."

Cuthbert looked disappointed. "Well, can you fit us in afterwards?" he asked hopefully.

The road gang examined the house from every angle, whilst Buster set up the striped tent.

Cuthbert wasn't fooled by all this posturing; it was to allow time for a crowd to gather.

The drains inspector addressed his men loudly enough for the audience to hear him. "Men," he began, "in my considered opinion, if we use high pressure hoses in the tunnels, the pressure will simply escape through the chimney."

The crowd oohed.

Percy flapped his arms. "We told him that!"

The drains inspector continued evenly, "Excessive heat in the kitchen area has increased the density of the material."

Percy flapped again. "We told him that too!"

"Shush, Percy," whispered Henry, "this is politics."

Percy jammed his lips together.

The drains inspector held up a hand dramatically. "Also," he said, "I have reason to believe there are creatures loose in the tunnels."

Percy fell flat on his back due to holding his breath.

The crowd began taking photographs as the road gang began to don protective gear and check equipment.

Avril appeared with her own photographer- this was dramatic stuff! She was composing the headline as she scribbled furiously. "Wheat-based life form takes over house from witless owner," she muttered.

"Cuthbert has been given his daily bread, now who will deliver us from evil?" The locals crowded around her tried to help.

Henry said, "We've already done 'farmhouse loaf'."

The Captain added, "We've had 'Cottage loaf' as well, dear."

Ronald contributed, "You can repeat the bit about the neighbourhood improving, now that the goats have moved in though!"

Marvin arrived just in time. Pushing his way through, he took command. "Well done, drains inspector," he began. "Done the simple preparations, I see. I'll take over now." He addressed the crowd directly. "Stand back everyone," he shouted, using his hands as an invisible megaphone. "The professionals are here. This is where your taxes go!"

Percy staggered to his feet just as Henry nudged him. "See Percy, Politics!"

Swivelling Simon adjusted his face mask. Why did the glass over his good eye always steam up and never the other one?

One lung Louie tested his breathing apparatus. One good whiff of oxygen invigorated him so much he could have sliced the house in two and made a sandwich.

Buster was slightly unconventional in his approach. His overalls were standard, but with the arms cut off to allow the muscles to ripple, and he tied a sweat band around his head.

The crowd whooped, clapped and cheered as the team stepped into the house.

Percy shrieked, "Why? We walk in there every day. What's so special?"

The crowd became hushed as if the bomb disposal team had gone in.

One lung Louie came out gasping.

The crowd sighed.

Simon appeared and helped Louie to get a shot of oxygen and Buster posed in the doorway guarding the scene.

Louie recovered and the team waved bravely as they went back in.

The crowd cheered, the women were swooning. Percy was furious. He took to shaking people by the lapels and screaming, "It's bread! They're fighting bread!" Then he reached Arkle and she threw him into the duck pond.

Inside the house, the team had scooped out a nice cosy area and sat discussing the job.

Swivelling Simon said, "Some of those women have caught my eye."

Louie offered, "That Margery makes me quite breathless."

Buster shook his head in wonder. "We've never been admired before. I didn't realise that this job could be glamorous."

The drains inspector struggled through the tunnel and flopped down beside them. "You've made a good impression out there lads," he gasped.

Buster swelled with pride. "I'll say" he agreed. "Someone asked for my autograph."

The others gaped in envy, until the drains inspector said, "That was Marvin; it was an overtime form."

Chapter Eight

Cuthbert wandered around his outbuildings; he didn't do that very often in case he found someone he had forgotten to bury.

Another night in Percy's shed was out of the question and he looked for alternative accommodation.

The old theatre was too draughty and most of the out-buildings were full of unrecognisable things only worth having if you knew what they were.

Emptying a set of shelves, Cuthbert briefly wondered if he could sleep on there like a bunk bed. Pulling boxes off the shelf, he noticed a door appearing on the back wall, so he emptied the whole stack of shelves. Pulling the shelf unit away, Cuthbert studied the door and realised he was not alone. "Have you just stood there and watched me move all those boxes?" he demanded.

"Yup!" said Percy.

Cuthbert looked at him accusingly. "Sometimes I think you are scared of hard work."

Percy was affronted. "No I'm not," he replied. "If I was scared of it, why would I stand so close watching *you* do it?"

The door was old. The lock and the hinges were rusty. Cuthbert ran around finding hammers, crowbars and anything else to gently smash it open. Staggering back, laden with tools, he found Percy sitting on a box, staring into the open doorway. Cuthbert dropped the tools with a clatter and spluttered, "What, where, how, when?"

Percy held up a rusty old key and hung it back on its nail near the door.

Cuthbert joined him on the box. "Have you been inside?" he whispered.

Percy shook his head.

"There you are!" boomed the Captain, making Percy and Cuthbert jump.

"We thought you'd eloped," quipped Henry.

Ronald sauntered in behind them and said, "Sat on a box in the dark, eh? That should have been the first place we looked."

The newcomers paused when they saw the door and realised this was a moment of importance.

36

"Who is going in first? It's your farm, Cuthbert," said Henry.

Ronald muttered, "Yes send him in first, the rest of us have lives to lead."

Cuthbert rose and took a lantern down from another shelf. After several attempts to light it, Ronald handed him one with a wick in it. Cuthbert moved forward in the eerie yellow glow; the rest followed, each holding a lantern.

The tunnel was made from stone with an arched roof. It was like the older sections found under the Valley.

Cuthbert rounded a bend. The space opened up before him into a room with a long table running down the middle and five old chairs around it. Some kind of primitive fireplace stood in the corner. The sudden draught ruffled the dust and flicked the pages of an old pamphlet.

The men grouped around the table and Henry had a sudden insight. "Close your eyes and choose your places," he said.

Each of them moved to a different chair.

At the place chosen by Ronald, the old pamphlet proclaimed, "Ye sword techniques" and an old sword lay beside it, the blade rusted away and only the hilt remaining.

The Captain found himself sat with an old dark green wine bottle and Percy had a page from 'Ye herbalists' notes.'

Henry studied the curved clay pipe at his place and Cuthbert fell over, because one chair leg was shorter than the other.

"It's as if we have all been here before," declared Percy as the paper page crumbled in his hand.

"We're certainly sitting in the right places," noted Ronald watching Cuthbert struggle to his feet.

The drains inspector warned his team. "Watch out for that Marvin," he said. "He's out there taking the credit for everything and it will be his report on the Mayor's desk."

Sitting back, the team listened to him politely. Even when a goat ate its way into their cavern, skipped over Louie's legs and ate its way out again, they still listened.

"Right then, lads, what are we going to do about this lot?" The drains inspector indicated his surroundings with a wave of his hands.

37

Jasper sat in his room with his head in his hands.

The voice from the other side of the door was saying, "Thith ith an anonymouth warning, Jathper. You will never know who thith ith and if you don't co-operate, I will tell your Mum!"

How had the leader of the Valley mafia landed in this situation, he asked himself.

Girls were for taking the blame and hiding behind. When the twins and Margery ran the Valley, this would never have happened.

He straightened. Margery- why hadn't he thought of that before?

Henry was in his element; he was convinced this was a secret meeting chamber from the days of the civil war where Cavaliers met to discuss tactics to defeat the Roundheads and restore the throne. "It's like the council meetings which took place under an ornate ceiling in London," he declared. "The ceiling boss was a carved rose and everything said beneath it was declared secret. Hence the Latin term 'Sub-Rosa'."

Ronald glanced up warily and asked, "Or 'sub-cobweb' in this case?"

The Captain was equally taken with the discovery. "But can we really believe that our ancestors gathered here in this very room and now we've re-discovered it?" He added, "Some of us don't even come from these parts."

Henry shrugged, there were no real answers.

"Besides," added Ronald, "it looks as if Percy's ancestor could read."

Margery was really rather touched. Jasper sat in a corner of the bar, pouring out his troubles over an orange juice.

Even Margery understood the inherent danger in pigtails and freckles. She patted Jaspers hand. "All women, of all ages need to feel wanted. Make her feel important, find her something to do. Make sure she only reports back to you." She patted his hand again. "Don't forget, Jasper, we women are satellites, we need something to orbit around."

Jasper entered the bar as a small, confused young man. He left it as a small, confused, slightly older young man.

"Come on, lads," urged the drains inspector, "the goats are doing a good job, but they're erratic. It will take months. What are *we* going to do?"

Swivelling Simon rolled his good eye to take in the scale of the problem. "Water," he suggested. "Straight down the chimney. Make it dissolve."

"No!" scoffed Louie, "It would go all pappy and stick together again. "We need to bash it into dust and suck it out!"

The drains inspector looked at Buster. "What do you fancy?"

"Toast," was the reply.

"Not for supper, lad; how do we solve this?"

Buster became animated. "No, really, toast, watch!" He pulled out a cigarette lighter and began flicking it.

The rest of the team cringed into a corner all trying to be the furthest away from the flames.

Buster held the flame up to the bread ceiling and watched it scorch. When it turned black, he put out the lighter and scratched away at the black mark. The bread crumbled into crumbs and drifted to the floor. "See?" he asked his cowering mates. "*Now* we can suck it out."

The team prepared for a dramatic exit. Donning full protection gear, they staggered out of the house. Unable to hear the cheering crowd through the thick smoke masks, they pantomimed helping Louie into the open and flopping to the ground gratefully.

There was no one there.

The fickle Valley folk had already forgotten them and wandered off. Perhaps the wind had changed and they had all gone off to watch the weathervane.

Pearl was braiding her dolly's hair when Jasper poked his head around her door. "Are you busy?" he asked nonchalantly.

"No," replied Pearl sarcastically. "Dolly'th quantum theory is weak tho. I'm doing thith to tighten her brain up."

Jasper gritted his teeth. *Satellite, eh,* he thought. If only he could find a rocket. Patiently, he explained that he needed someone trustworthy for a special mission. That person would have to report only to him.

Pearl's feminine curiosity was engaged and the flattery made the

39

words go all fuzzy, so that her common sense became blurred. She was hooked.

The group sat around the ancient table, shadows lengthening and shortening as the lanterns flickered.

The Captain asked what matter of great moment would be discussed by the secret group tonight. The assembly thought for a while and Cuthbert asked, "Are we doing any baking for this contest?"

Henry's chair crashed back against the wall and a startled Cuthbert fell over again. Henry stood, his shadow curving over them due to the vaulted ceiling and he roared, "*Baking, baking*! Our ancestors sat where we are now, plotting to restore the King to his throne. They made their pledges and vouchsafed their blood. *They were men* and the enemy was at the gates!" Henry's fist crashed against the unyielding oak of the table and brought him to his senses. "Sorry, chaps," he spluttered, "got a bit carried away there for a moment." Then, rubbing his hand, he sat.

Percy leaned over to Ronald and whispered, "Meetings can get a bit heated in this rosy submarine thing, can't they?"

Chapter Nine

Next morning, Elspeth had fed Percy and they sat enjoying the silence, when there was a knock on the door.

Percy opened it and a little girl walked in. She wore a pink gingham dress and had pig-tails and freckles.

Elspeth was immediately charmed and began feeding her all the fancy cakes deemed to be too good for Percy.

After thoroughly ingratiating herself and lisping sweetly to 'Elthpeth' she had succeeded in getting close to 'the scruffy one'.

Percy wasn't fooled for a moment. Anything dressed like this that wasn't a fairground prize, was highly suspicious in his eyes.

"Oh, Percy," said Elspeth, "just chat to sweet little Pearl for a moment, while I take these cakes out of the oven, will you?"

Percy leant across the table and whispered to Pearl. Elspeth stood and placed a fresh tray of cakes on the table. Pearl stood watching.

"There," said Elspeth. "Did you and Percy have a nice chat?"

"Oh, yeth," replied Pearl. "He taught me a new thong."

"Which one was that, dear?" asked Elspeth.

Pearl screwed up her face in concentration and replied, "Thing a thong of thixthpence, Elthpeth."

Elspeth looked up sharply, but Percy's chair was empty.

The road gang queued in Mrs Biggle's Post Office. She had refused to sell Buster five cigarette lighters and now they had to queue. "Next," called Mrs Biggle, peering through the mesh screen.

The drains inspector stepped up and asked to buy a cigarette lighter. "Are you over sixteen?" she asked.

"Oh, yes," assured the drains inspector.

"Do you know smoking can kill?" she snapped next.

"Er, yes, I believe it can," stuttered the hapless man.

"Why do you do it then?" demanded the post mistress.

"But I don't," the drains inspector assured her.

Mrs Biggle's expression became fierce. "Why do you want them lighters then?"

The drains inspector's quick wit stalled quite appallingly as he said, "To toast Cuthbert's house."

Shrill cries of "Arson, police, police!" sent the men scurrying out of the shop, accompanied by clouds of 'peach blossom' compact powder.

Gathering outside to regroup, Buster adopted his 'I told you so' expression and Simon spoke up. "Why don't we buy them from someone else?" he asked.

The drains inspector scoffed. "Who, for instance?"

Simon replied with a directional nod, "Well, that kid with a tray around his neck looks promising."

Jasper sold ten cigarette lighters to the disgruntled team for three times the cost of the ones in the Post Office.

The road gang grumbled off into the distance and Jasper popped into the Post Office to give Mrs Biggle her percentage.

"Well done, dear," she said. "Do you think they'll be back?"

Jasper accepted a lollipop and replied, "Oh yes, they work much better with gas inside them," and he rattled the refills on his tray.

"I don't like that Perthy!" snapped Pearl. "I can't get that thong out of my head and I've been thpitting on my dolly all day thinging it."

Jasper had to admire Percy's grasp of tactics, but he reassured Pearl that he needed to know Percy and Cuthbert's movements and she was the best operative for the job. "The whole mission could collapse without you," he confided.

"What ith the mithion?" she asked.

Jasper tapped the side of his nose. "Need to know basis," he said archly, "need to know," and went to his room.

Pearl watched him go with narrowed eyes. *You need your nothe all right,* she thought, *and if you're not careful, thothe armth will be coming off too, mate.*

Once the road gang had paid through the nose and assembled the lighters, they began to clear Cuthbert's house.

One lung-Louie found it a bit dusty, so he sat outside in the road sweeper. The rubber hose pulsated as it snaked into the front door and sucked out the toast dust.

Buster and Swivelling Simon worked away at the 'Toast-Face'

42

chucking the spoil behind them like dogs looking for a bone. They worked so fast that the tunnel behind them began to fill up. Either production beat the road sweeper hose, or Louie had fallen asleep again.

The wall before them suddenly crumbled and fell away. A stone tunnel stretched ahead and the way back was blocked.

Avril chewed at her fingernail again. "It must be a scoop, it must be," she insisted to herself.

The litter bin was buried under a pile of paper pom-poms thrown with great accuracy until a pyramid had formed.

Avril tore another piece of paper out from the typewriter, crumpled it and launched it across the room.

She had been using the computer all morning, but it became illogically annoyed at her changing demands and whatever motivated it seemed to have closed its windows, opened its doors and fled. The first time in weeks when the Valley cables held enough strength to power the thing and it had a hissy-fit.

Avril gave her fingernail a rest and chewed her lip instead. "Local undertaker bakes himself out of a home," she muttered to herself as she typed. "Local oaf uses his loaf," she tried. Sitting back, she gazed out of her window onto the never changing street. *There's no wonder nobody knows about this place,* she thought. *Even when something happens, the news just can't get out.*

Cuthbert had finished his project. He stood back to admire his handiwork. The sheep version of Marilyn Monroe gazed back at him affectionately. Being the local undertaker, Cuthbert had to keep his skills polished.

The butcher in the next valley would send a spare sheep's head over now and again, so that he could practice his make-up techniques.

Percy was outside pottering with his tractor, so Cuthbert lifted 'Marilyn' and carried her outside. "Hey, Percy," shouted Cuthbert, holding the head up. "Give us a kiss!"

The high pitched scream could only just be heard by man, but blind-Pugh hid his head under his kennel several hundred yards away.

Cuthbert had a fleeting impression of something pink and white with pig-tails hurtling away from him at high speed and Percy slicking his hair down and pursing his lips.

That afternoon, Jasper appeared at the farm. He shook Cuthbert's hand until a sympathetic vibration made Cuthbert quiver.

Percy was given similar treatment as Jasper enthused, "She's gone, she's gone. Thank you, thank you," he said.

Cuthbert raised both hands palms outward to say, "It was nothing, whatever *it* was."

Jasper yelled, "Yeah, high five," and slapped Cuthbert's palm.

Percy held his hands up before he was attacked too and Jasper slapped his hand in the same manner.

Jasper went away whistling and waving back at them.

"High five?" asked Percy, looking at his stinging palm.

"Yeah," shouted Cuthbert, and they went for an enthusiastic slap, missed and tied their arms in a Yorkshire knot.

The drains inspector had been following some of the goat tunnels to try to work out how much work was still to be done. Crawling about on hands and knees wasn't to be recommended at his age, especially when a corner turned often meant a goat met.

Returning to the kitchen area where he had left Simon and Buster working away, he was shocked to find that the room was full again. *Roof-fall*, he thought and he scrambled out to get help.

Louie had just switched the road sweeper off as the gauge was showing 'Full'.

The drains inspector came over wild-eyed and shouting for him to phone the rescue team immediately.

"We *are* the rescue team," Louie pointed out.

The drains inspector was taken aback. "But what happens if the rescue team needs rescuing?"

Louie rubbed his chin, "Ah, now that would involve 'Maddie'.

The drains inspector blinked. "Who's Maddie?"

Louie took a deep and yet still insignificant breath, before explaining, "**M**ajor **A**ccident & **D**esignated **D**isaster **I**ncident **E**chelon."

The drains inspector flapped his arms, "Well, where do we find

44

them?"

Louie stared at the floor and replied, "That's us too, after the last budget cuts. It was either an additional team or smaller offices for the Mayor and his staff. We lost."

Buster led the way along the tunnel. His cap-lamp beam sweeping the way ahead.

Simon followed quietly behind.

Tunnels were second nature to them and as there were no obvious perils lurking, it was quite interesting really.

The drains inspector had grabbed a young lad who happened to be sitting on the stile watching them. Unfortunately, the young lad was the martial arts instructor to the Valley mafia and head-locks were his speciality.

After Louie and the drains inspector gaspingly explained the situation, the young lad went off to raise the alarm.

Soon a chain gang was formed and buckets were being passed backwards as most of the Valley worked to clear the fall.

Cuthbert and Percy managed to dig in a slightly different direction to everyone else. They were dying for a cuppa.

Buster and Simon had entered a curved vault with a ladder reaching upwards.

Simon had seen one of these before. "It's an ice-house," he explained. "The meat and vegetables would be stored in here with blocks of ice. This was the farm's freezer before fridges were even thought of. You simply came through the tunnel for anything you needed."

Buster was more interested in climbing the ladder and he soon disappeared upwards.

Simon followed; his eye was starting to stick in the cold air.

Arriving back at the road sweeper, Buster and Simon found a hive of activity.

People were frantically passing buckets back down a line of people and throwing them into the duck pond.

45

At the front of the line, the situation was simply seen as "Two grown men are buried under a pile of breadcrumbs," but thanks to the Valley folk and their Shakespearean need to dramatize everything, at the back of the line, where Buster asked what was happening, the situation was revealed as, "Several children are trapped under a roof-fall. The whole Valley has collapsed on them."

Buster and Simon raced for the road sweeper cab. Grabbing their emergency helmets and face masks, they pushed past the line of helpers who burst into spontaneous applause at the appearance of a rescue team.

The drains inspector almost fainted with relief as the two professionally clad men forced their way to the front and began to work like demons. He sat gratefully and took a rest. After a while, he began to wonder who they were.

One of them seemed to have a faulty face mask. The eyes were moving in different directions.

Cuthbert and Percy walked back out into the farmyard. Shoulders were slumped and shovels were dragging behind them. The people at the back of the line feared the worst.

"Oh, the poor little dears," sobbed Mrs Biggle.

Avril was hit by emotions from all directions. Here she was, at the scene of a major tragedy, notebook in hand. This was Pulitzer Prize territory. *Hold all emotion back,* she told herself, *be objective, but wring every ounce of pathos out of every word.*

She approached Cuthbert who seemed very close to tears.

Even Percy's eyes were lack-lustre.

Avril adopted a sympathetic tone as she asked, "Is it as bad as we feared?"

Cuthbert paused and nodded slowly. "Probably worse," he began. "The cooking range has gone out; it is stone cold." He shambled away.

The drains inspector drew himself painfully to his feet and grabbed one of the rescue team by the shoulder, turning him in the process. One eye rolled alarmingly.

"*Is that you, Simon?*" screamed the drains inspector.

Avril watched her dreams crumble, just like the apple pie she had secretly attempted last night. One minute she had felt the heat of the international spotlight on her and now she watched people throwing buckets at each other. She went from being 'The intrepid young reporter who risked all for her story' to 'a twerp who didn't have two men buried in bread-crumbs.'

Cuthbert and Percy surveyed the cooking range. It was like looking at a corpse. All the fire and malice had gone out of it and if left, it would rust away into dust.

"Can we get it going again?" asked Percy.

Cuthbert shrugged. "I don't know. I've never seen it go out before."

Percy opened doors and peered into openings. Half the kitchen had been cleared. The huge table and chairs were still buried, but Percy was upbeat. "We may have lost this dump," he said, "but we can always move into the 'nice house' the road gang found.

Cuthbert sighed. "*Ice house,* Percy, *ice house.*"

Percy muttered, "That's what I said."

Old newspapers were rolled up and thrust into the bowels of the cooking range, along with pieces of wood and any dry debris to assist combustion. Buckets of coal were on stand-by and some strange looking fire-lighters Percy insisted upon moulding into 'snowmen' before putting them inside.

The moment came and a small wisp of smoke appeared, curled around itself and went out.

After several failures, Percy lost patience and threw in some paraffin and his last match. The whoomf sound and its accompanying flame cleared the rest of the kitchen of crumbs, dust and spiders, and the table was revealed again.

The cooking range began to make rumbling noises and expanding metal supplied an accompanying clicking sound. They now had a kitchen and an ice house.

Upstairs was still blocked, but the goats continued to chew that problem over.

At last, the kettle was boiled and the table clear. Percy sat with his feet up on another chair and Cuthbert tried to do the same with Arkle's

47

'loaf'. "Ooh, look Percy, it's gone all soft."

"Well, wear thicker socks," muttered Percy dreamily, enjoying the moment.

Cuthbert peeled a piece off the lump. The extra flash of heat must have been just what Arkle's 'roadblock' needed.

Percy opened one eye to find Cuthbert moulding shapes and rolling flat sheets of dough all over the table.

"Missing the nursery, are we?" he asked.

Cuthbert ignored him because it was the only way to guarantee getting Percy's attention.

Eventually, when Percy moved closer and began rolling balls of dough himself, Cuthbert said, "We've got the biggest oven in the Valley and a year's supply of dough. Why don't *we* bake something?"

Percy laughed. "Like what?"

Cuthbert thought. "Well, how hard can it be? They roll out a sheet of this stuff, put something inside and lay another sheet on top."

Percy became interested. "What shall we put in it then?"

Cuthbert spoke confidently. "Anything you like, mate, then we give it an exotic name and Bob's your uncle."

"Granddad," said Percy absently.

"Pardon?" asked Cuthbert.

Percy looked up. "Bob was my granddad. Reggie was my uncle."

Cuthbert stared at him. "Last time I said that, you said something different."

"No, I didn't," said Percy, carefully denying something he wasn't sure of.

Cuthbert insisted, "Yes, you did, but I can't remember what it was."

Percy pounced. "Neither can I, so how do we know we're having this argument?"

They quietly rolled and moulded for a while and the next time anyone spoke, it was a different subject entirely.

"Pass me an apple, please, Cuthbert," requested Percy.

"Certainly," replied Cuthbert. "Can you spare some of that bacon?"

The road gang had just about exhausted the blame game. Buster and Simon were the victims of an underground phenomenon, the drains

48

inspector should have been supervising properly and it was all Louie's fault anyway, because he fell asleep. Once they got their breath back, it would start again and the roles would be reversed. The office wasn't as pristine as it had been, but at least crumbs could be swept up.

"Ta-DA!" crowed Cuthbert as he dragged a steaming tray out of the oven. Several little mounds had browned nicely. He sniffed deeply at the aromas of fresh baking and cooked meat. Then he realised that his fingers were burning and put the tray down to bathe his hands.

Percy dragged his tray out suspiciously. All his offerings lay flat, but they were brown. Tray after tray was pulled out and laid out on the long table.

The guests were starting to arrive and the tasting could begin.

Avril took a seat and resigned herself to obscurity. If she wasn't going to be famous, then she might as well be fat. Lifting a cover, she gasped, "*Is that a tail Percy?*"

Percy looked over. "Could be," he said. "That's fisherman's pie, that is."

The women huddled together at one end of the table and watched in awe.

Cuthbert presented an apple pie. It was round like a cricket ball and had a stalk sticking out of the top.

The men were really impressed; the centre piece was a 'game pie' with little footballers stuck on top.

Percy unveiled his 'bacon bakes' and explained they were "bacon sandwiches without using bread."

Cuthbert rivalled this with a 'Rice crispies' cake swimming in milk.

The vegetarian section had been Percy's inspiration. Whatever was in it had stained the pastry green and now it looked like his beloved 'Kryptonite'.

The women held their throats, the men licked their lips and Arkle sighed, "If only my dough turned out like that!"

People went away with samples of every type and promised to report back with their findings. The way some of the women held things at arm's length impressed Percy. "Don't want to bruise the apples, see!" he said.

49

The Captain and Henry were rather fascinated with the meeting room. Though Cuthbert had his kitchen back, they liked to just sit and enjoy the silence and speculate about the schemes and plots this room must have heard over the years.

Ronald had joined them tonight because, as he put it, "I'm not sitting with head-chef and head-case on my own." They sat in silence with only candles for light. The atmosphere seemed loaded with intrigue. Ronald suddenly asked, "I wonder if this place was used for witchcraft?"

The other two quickly dismissed his question, but somehow the shadows seemed to deepen.

Ronald persisted. "Ideal place, you know. Tucked away underground where no-one can hear the screams."

Henry and the Captain looked at each other and scoffed in stereo.

Ronald held up his hand. "Don't be so hasty. I've seen things, you know. This is a lot like the caves where strange things happened at night. Drumming, chanting and in the end ... a scream."

Henry and the Captain sat a little bit straighter. It seemed cold in there somehow and Cuthbert's kitchen was warm. The scrape of stone on stone petrified all three of them. They had no sooner focused on the block sliding out of the wall than a sudden draught blew the candles out.

The three men found themselves scrabbling at the exit door. It was stuck.

Around the corner in the room they had just left, a glow showed around the wall. A rumbling sound came next and then a hiss. "Oh, good Lord, snakes," said the Captain.

"Nerve gas!" suggested Ronald.

Henry couldn't put a positive spin on either of those, so he kept quiet. Another hiss! It was closer this time; there was only one course of action open to them.

"We all rush in together," whispered Ronald. "Whatever it is; we tackle it together."

They all nodded uselessly in the dark and, holding hands, they rushed around the corner to be met by the most violent hiss yet.

Cuthbert and Percy sat at a table groaning with goodies. They had tried

50

everything and new combinations were coming all the time. Cuthbert's beetroot and onion looked like being an acquired taste and it was put in the vegetarian section.

However, Percy's 'Coq-au-vin' pie was simply splendid. It took a lot of pastry, but standing there in the centre of the table, it looked like a life sized model. Percy had polished its beak, straightened its comb and put tooth-picks in-between its claws. You could almost expect it to crow, except that three-quarters of an hour in Cuthbert's cooking range tended to quieten most things down.

"Hello, boys, hope I didn't disturb you," said a sweet voice behind a pressurised can of polish.

Ronald writhed on the ground holding his face, Henry stared in disbelief and the Captain said, "Elspeth! What are you doing here?"

Elspeth gave the chair a last flick with her duster and replied, "Oh, Marjorie found this place on her wanderings. She said there was a dusty old table down here and I have only just got around to it." She looked accusingly at her husband and said, "I don't just spend my life dusting, you know."

The Captain led his wife back the way she had come and as she left, she turned to Ronald and said, "Ooh, that's made your nose all shiny, Ronald."

Henry and Ronald sat quietly around Cuthbert's table until the Captain joined them.

Gradually, the story came out and Percy started rearranging the feathers on his 'Cock Pie' as he had christened it. He loved anything which involved embarrassing Ronald and the distraction was the only way he could stop laughing.

Henry recalled the way the block of stone had simply slid out and dropped on the floor and Percy said, "That's standard, that is. Lots of my ancestors were stone masons and that's how they disguised the priest holes and secret passages."

Ronald nodded towards the 'cock pie' and offered, "By the looks of that thing, they must have come up with some bonny buildings."

Percy patted his pie on the head to comfort it and added, "My ancestors had a hand in most of the cathedrals in England."

51

Ronald suggested, "Had a hand in most of the tills in England, more like."

Percy ignored him, sat, and shuffled. After their recent experience with a spray polish, the men seemed quite happy just to sit with other people, so they sat still and tried to tear their eyes away from Percy's gruesome cock-pie.

"Stone-masons were the bees-knees in medieval England," began Percy. "They could name their own price. Did I mention that my ancestor invented the 'Plumm-Line' to show when something is vertical? Anyway, my relative was the master mason in charge of this new cathedral and he wanted to try out a new shape. The church didn't agree, because they were more interested in acoustics and splendour than advanced architecture. My ancestor built it just the way they wanted and the acoustics were perfect. After all the chanting and testing was over and my ancestor was paid, he took his team back in and they removed several false stone walls by taking out the middle block and dismantling it from the middle. By the time they had done, it was exactly how my ancestor had wanted it in the first place. Everybody gathered for the first service and official blessing and even the King was present. Everyone was amazed at the internal structure, they had never seen anything like it and everyone wanted to know who was responsible. He had built many Cathedrals, but they all looked the same, so this would be the making of my ancestor. He would be able to put his name on the side of his carts and get all the big contracts."

Percy paused for breath. "The Bishops were convinced that something had changed, but they didn't know what, so they went ahead with an inaugural 'blood and thunder' sermon. Now, by taking down the interior walls, it had in fact altered the acoustics. It slowed down the delivery of the sermon by cutting the echoes short. The people on the outside edge got the message slightly after anyone in the middle, and some bits were actually missing because they met other echoes coming back and they cancelled each other out! So, when the Bishop roared, 'Do you covet your neighbour's wife? Well, you can't have her!' The people on the outer walls heard, 'You can have her.' The congregation on the outside looked at each other and then at each other's wives."

Clearly, Percy warmed to his own tale. "When the Bishop repeated it, there were knives drawn! Some were defending their wives and others were looking for a bargain. One of the passages lost in the echo was, 'But if you do, you will be condemned to eternity in hell, which became, 'And you can continue in hell.' The Bishop then yelled, 'Do you covet the rich man's clothing? Well, you can't have it!' and the same effect produced, 'Well, you can have it. By now, there were people without clothes who didn't know whether they were being coveted or robbed, or whether they had just joined a fraternity or eternity. The people in the middle of the cathedral realised that all the fun was being had on the outer edges and dashed to join in. My ancestor was quite quick on the uptake and he made a run for it in the confusion."

Percy grinned. "The cathedral was declared cursed and torn down. That's why there are so many Cathedral ruins in Britain and a failed builder was said to be 'Plumm out of luck!'"

Chapter Ten

Margery tapped her manicured nails on the bar top. The rest of the women sat watching Cuthbert and Percy's baking as if it was about to give birth. Margery sighed, stopped tapping and asked, "What on earth do we tell the boys?"

Arkle suggested, "Tell them we left it outside and blind-Pugh ate it."

All heads shook together. Even a blind sheep dog wasn't going to fall for this lot.

Margery poked the top of Percy's 'Salmonella surprise' with the edge of a beer mat. *That fish really did not look dead,* she thought.

The whole room seemed to be waiting for her lead, so she sighed yet again and *stared*. "Elspeth!" she shrieked, "What are you doing?"

Chairs scraped back as the assembly saw Elspeth sample a piece of pastry. Elspeth chewed daintily and swallowed in her own time. "Have any of you actually tried this pastry?" she asked. "It's really rather good."

Nervous eyes and reluctant fingers were gradually replaced by smiles and sounds of appreciation. It *was* rather good. The trick was to ignore the monstrosities lurking beneath it.

The whole meeting became electrified. Questions flew back and forth, but the answers refused to appear.

Margery suddenly mentioned the unmentionable. "It's not out of a packet, is it?" Glancing to one side, she asked, "Avril?"

Avril stopped licking her fingers and replied, "Oh no, definitely not," and then paused suspiciously to ask, "Why did you ask *me* that?"

The crow had never been a material kind of bird; not much room in a nest for collections of antiques or large sound systems. If ever he needed a special glittering gift, he visited the magpies' emporium with a fat worm.

His only weakness was fresh baking. The smell seemed to concentrate over the Valley and then spread out until it found him. It had found him today all right.

He had been living upstairs in the dopey one's house since it

54

turned into a loaf overnight. Every time he ate a meal, his living space got bigger, it was great.

True, he had to avoid the scruffy one and a couple of goats now and again and he was pretty sick of bread too by now.

The smell had seeped between the cracks and gaps to find him and he was drawn into the goat shaped tunnels to investigate. According to the laws of crow-dom, it was 'always move down to feed and up to escape', so down he went. The tunnels were puzzling, the dozy goats often crossed each other's paths, but he kept going down regardless until he came to an open space.

He seemed to be in some sort of temple. Right in the middle, was a life sized effigy of a bird. At first, he thought he had stumbled upon the legendary 'Temple of the Great Crow' but the comb on the head was a bit of a giveaway.

This must be the tomb of the Great Chicken, he thought. Apparently, that's why chickens were always dipping their heads to the ground. It was to salute the Tomb of the Great Chicken, but because no-one knew where it was, they saluted in all different directions, just to make sure. Someone seemed to know where it was though, as offerings were laid out in front of it, *baking*.

The crow tripped along the table from dish to dish. *There were some very strange looking delicacies here*, he thought. (From someone who sampled anything left anywhere by anyone, it was *some* observation). The crow was slightly uneasy in this room; the chicken's eyes seemed to follow him around. The crow studied the chicken. By cocking his head from side to side, he could use one side of his brain after the other. If he did it too fast, he simply fell over. The chicken seemed to be embalmed in pastry. It made sense that the head chicken would only be encased in the finest pastry ever made, so the crow tried a bit, then a bit more. This really was the finest pastry he had ever tasted. The delicate sample became a very unbecoming tussle between hungry crow and a late chicken. The crow wasn't very pleased; in fact, he was literally spitting feathers. *Surely,* he thought, *it is wise to shave something before you embalm it?*

A clattering in the tunnel alerted him to the approach of one of the goats. He didn't like goats, they were expressionless.

The crow ran to the door and stopped. The yard was full of chickens. *Oh no,* he thought, *trapped between a cock and a hard-face.*

These must be the guardians of the temple, *probably trained*

55

killers, he thought. Watching them for a moment, he noticed that they were still dipping their heads in all directions even though they were right outside the temple door; no doubt a crafty ruse to throw grave-robbers off the scent.

The crow checked behind him and the goat was watching with interest. Perhaps he was sick of eating bread too.

The crow strutted into the yard dipping his head because his life depended on it. He had enough feather and pastry mix stuck to him to mingle amongst them without causing too much excitement. All he needed now was a cover story in case he was questioned.

The road gang were despondent. There was a smudge on the carpet and nobody cared. Tools were propped up in a corner and still nobody cared. They had enjoyed their moment of fame, but they quickly learnt the truth of these things. Fame was fleeting and if you hadn't booked it for a certain time, it would come and go without you.

The drains inspector tried to cheer them up. "Come on, lads! We're still the Local Authority's Secret Service," he reminded them.

"Only because they're ashamed of us," muttered Buster.

They all knew this was true and the room fell silent.

Simon suggested, "We could always bury Louie, wait for the excitement to build and then dig him up again." He cast a glance across the room, but Louie wasn't reacting- he was asleep again.

Avril stared at the phone. She let it ring for a while to make sure it was serious and then picked it up.

Her boss asked whether "Anything had happened this week?"

Avril assured him that lots of things had happened.

"Good, good," he said. "Write them up, girl, write them up," and he hung up.

Avril stared at the receiver in disbelief. Did he know where she worked? The world could end overnight in the Valley, but by the time the locals had done with it, there would be nothing to report. The frustrated young reporter put her head in her hands and stared at the desk top.

Behind her, a sombre procession wound its way through the high street. The temple guards carried the remains of the Great Chicken to a new and safer resting place. They hadn't even known that he was there until the strange prophet had appeared and informed them of their loss.

The last drooping tail feather had rounded the corner just as Avril spun around in her chair and stared hopelessly into the street. *I need some news,* she thought. *Out of all these eccentrics bumbling around like random atomic particles, surely some of them will collide and do something interesting?* Picking up her notebook she went outside.

Percy slammed his way happily into the kitchen, just in front of Cuthbert. "Where's my 'Coq-au-vin'?" he yelled. Scooping up piles of discarded feathers, he glared around. "Flaming goats!"

Constable Beeching was having trouble sleeping. There was only one thing that could possibly interfere with his sleep and that was eating. His dreams had been particularly realistic lately and they had woken him up. Even the cells were full of the smell of baking. This had become serious, he would have to investigate.

Margery dusted the bar rather vigorously, hoping she could knock some of the pies off onto the floor. They seemed to be welded to the wood. Turning, she concentrated on polishing the optics on the wall.

Suddenly, a shadow fell across the bar and Constable Beeching's voice came clearly. "Ooh, bar snacks," he said.

Margery smiled. "Care for a drink on the house, Constable?" she asked sweetly.

Percy had wandered into town looking for exotic ingredients for his next culinary creations. He saw Avril peep round the corner of her office and scribble something in her notebook. When he reached the Post Office, he pretended to bend down and adjust his welly. Sure enough, Avril was watching him from another angle.

He straightened up and pulled out a tatty old notebook. Licking the end of a pencil, he studied the front of the building and made notes. Then he paced out the width of the building and made more notes. He began tapping the walls and shaking his head before making more notes.

Avril watched in fascination. There had always been something

57

odd about Percy. *Nobody,* she thought, *could be that dim and survive.*

Then she remembered Cuthbert. *She* was forgetting where she worked now.

Percy finished scribbling on his piece of paper and after looking around furtively, he poked it into a crack in the Post Office wall. Then, taking a stub of chalk from a pocket, he scrawled a symbol on the floor nearby. With a last look around, he walked away whistling.

Avril was dumbfounded. She knew all about this tactic- it was called a 'dead letter box'. Spies left messages there for their contacts to pick up later. She had stumbled upon an espionage ring.

Writing furiously, she crept along in the shadows and retrieved the piece of paper. After copying it into her notebook, she replaced Percy's original and scuttled back to her office.

Back at her desk, Avril read Percy's message aloud. "The time is near, no-one suspects. This building has good locks to hold hostages."

Avril gaped. She read it again and gaped some more. Lots of adjectives queued up for insertion before Percy's name every time she had to use it, but 'dangerous' had never been one of them.

She reached for the phone, hesitated and put it down again. *What would a really intrepid reporter do,* she asked herself. She didn't actually know any, so it was back to guessing. Realising that the note was all she had, Avril made up her mind. She would stake out the dead letter box and take photographs of Percy and his accomplices.

Jasper sauntered across the road with his hands in his pockets. Stopping at the crack in the wall, he looked around furtively before removing the piece of paper.

Avril took a picture.

Jasper smiled to himself.

Mrs Biggle put down the phone. Percy seemed really worried about a crack in her Post Office wall. She sighed, didn't anyone realise how busy she was? Still, she had better check it out for herself.

Avril had positioned herself inside the old red pillar box.

Everyone handed their letters to Mrs Biggle because they had to buy a stamp anyway, so why walk across the street to post it?

Wriggling to get comfortable, she focused on Jasper, took the photo and started to write her notes. The sound of the bell over the Post Office door made her look through the slit.

Mrs Biggle came out onto the pavement and studied the crack closely. Then she spotted the chalk mark on the pavement. Tutting, she rubbed it off with the sole of her shoe thinking *blooming kids* and went back inside. *Did that post box just flash at me?*

Avril had to remind herself to breathe. *It is a conspiracy,* she thought. *Who else is involved?*

Just then, Percy appeared again, coming towards her.

Percy seemed agitated; he almost ran across to the crack in the Post Office wall and pushed something into it. Then he bent and applied another chalk mark on the pavement. Seeing the flash from the letter box, he casually crossed over the street.

Avril crouched lower as Percy approached. He came right over and leant against the post box. Avril could make out voices. She raised herself and put her ear to the letter slot.

Percy was saying, "She suspects, we may have to get rid of her."

Avril gulped. Another voice nearby asked, "Will anyone miss her?"

Percy snorted, "No. When did you last see a 'by-line' from a reporter working in this Valley? We always get to them before they can write it up."

Avril gulped again. The other voice said, "Time is of the essence, see to it quickly."

Percy replied, "Consider it done," and walked away.

Margery paused in the doorway of the Mandrake Arms. Percy seemed to be talking to himself. *No surprise there,* she thought, and then watched carefully as the door on the back of the pillar box creaked open.

She watched as Avril stepped out of the red box and sneaked across the street to the Post Office. Margery could see Avril take something out of a crack in the wall and run for her office.

A minute or two later, the blind was drawn over the huge window of the newspaper office and Avril had cut herself off.

Avril spoke breathlessly into a miniature tape recorder. This was a record of the events rapidly shaping up in the Valley. It might even be her last testament.

She laid out the first transcript from the crack in the wall and smoothed out the next communiqué at the side of it. It read, 'Post office vaporised - Land spacecraft as soon as local reporter cannot see the street - The earth is ours!'

59

Avril stared until the letters blurred. Her thoughts refused to form an orderly queue. *Spaceship, Percy, cannot see street, hostages.* "Just a minute," she said out loud, "I can always see the street."

She turned her swivel chair slowly and stared at the big green blind. How had they known that she would close the blind, what would she see when she opened it?

Avril's shaking hand reached for the cord to raise the blind; this may be the worst thing she had ever seen. She raised it; *there they were.* The whole Valley was grinning at her; with Percy right in the middle, squashing his nose against the glass.

She shook her head and lowered the blind with a thud. She was right; it *was* the worst thing she had ever seen.

Cuthbert was suspicious. Percy was distrustful.

The women had called round for a visit and they were trying hard to be nice.

Elspeth volunteered to make the tea and busied herself bullying the kitchen range.

Margery uncovered a plate of tarts and cookies.

Geraldine admired the beams and original features, but Arkle sat quietly looking around. It was as if she was looking for something.

Elspeth found the cups, but couldn't find anything to sterilise them with and Margery used a bread board for a plate.

Geraldine was all excited in a corner. She had found some authentic period graffiti, in chicken-scratch writing on some peeling wallpaper. Her excitement faded somewhat, as she read Cuthbert's shopping list.

Cuthbert and Percy watched everything silently. The trick with a woman was to stay quiet for long enough and the questions would just burst out. With this many women, it would be even quicker.

Arkle still hadn't found what she was looking for.

"The thing is, boys," said Margery, desperately trying to fill the silence supplied by the two men, "we may need some extra pastry when the big day comes; we wondered if either of you have any old recipes?"

Percy reluctantly stammered and swung his feet nervously. "Do you mean the recipe for 'Percy Plumm's Patent Plum Pudding Potion'?"

Margery paused. "I don't know dear, do I?"

Elspeth sat with the others and they shared the cup that Geraldine had brought to pretend to borrow sugar in.

The women leaned in as Percy shuffled and explained, "Well," he began, "that recipe was handed down through the family. We used to be bakers in London at the time of Charles the Second; great one for his tarts apparently," he added for historical interest. "The King used to come round to our place in Pudding Lane during the night and try some of the day's bake while it was fresh from the oven; then we would lower the shop front and sell the rest when it cooled. He was a regular visitor, he was. Some thought it was the buxom wench who mixed the dough who kept him coming back, but we knew it was the pastry."

Percy winked. "One night, he called in after some big shindig at the Mansion House and he was showing us why they called him 'The Merry Monarch' when the head baker noticed some sacks had been delivered by mistake. We thought we had plenty of flour, but it was gunpowder. Now, the state the King was in, he probably wouldn't have noticed, but the customers in the morning would. The only thing we could do was leave the King in charge and get some more flour from the custom's house."

"Anyway," Percy paused to check on his audience and Cuthbert slid away under the table, "while they were away, the King started showing off to the buxom wench and said he would show her how to make a royal sandwich. The girl had ambitions in catering, so she repaid the compliment by making him pancakes. Between the two of them, they blew the roof off the shop and set fire to half of London. The King went down in history as being one of the first on the scene, heroically trying to put out the fire and we got the blame."

Percy shook his head ruefully. "The fruit market burned down as well; 1666 was a terrible year for Plumms."

The women left the house in a daze. No-one said anything and Arkle was still looking around. She gave the impression that she'd be back.

Cuthbert sidled back into the room. "What was all that about?"

Percy shrugged. "Don't know," he said. "Some people just like history."

Cuthbert sighed. "Not that, all this interest in our pastry. Do you think they liked the pies we sent?"

Percy considered this. "Are they trying to steal our secrets?"

"Do we have any?" asked Cuthbert in return.

The two friends sat and thought, but with limited concentration skills, they were soon miles away from each other and any conclusion was buried deeper than 'The Great Chicken'.

The women were back in the Mandrake arms. Margery was pacing agitatedly. "They know something," she said. "Where did Cuthbert sneak off to?"

Geraldine mused, "They could be living in a treasure house, you know. A place that old must have secrets."

Elspeth had been wearing several pairs of rubber gloves before tackling Cuthbert's bio-hazard of a kitchen and she struggled to remove the last pair. "I don't understand it," she muttered. "You never see either of them with an ailment. Perhaps all the germs get stuck in the grease?"

Arkle had to repeat herself as her question refused to register with the domestic software fitted to the other women. "AHEM! Did anyone see *my pastry* at Cuthbert's?"

Elspeth's rubber glove gave a vicious 'snap' as her grip slipped. "Oh, my goodness" she gasped.

Geraldine closed her mouth as self-preservation overcame sarcasm.

Margery sat heavily. "You don't think, they couldn't, they haven't?" she stammered.

"How much have we got left?" Cuthbert asked.

Percy looked up and replied, "Oh, loads. I made new insoles for my wellies and there is still plenty." He waggled his feet with pleasure. "It slices up really thin with a sharp knife."

Cuthbert stroked his chin. His father always said it stimulated the blood flow to the brain, but all it did for Cuthbert was to give him the rash that shaving never would. "Perhaps we should hide it?" he suggested.

Percy shrugged, "Why? Arkle was sitting on it and never noticed."

Cuthbert conceded this was a good point. "That's a good point," he said.

Percy wasn't actually worried about the pastry. His problem was finding the exotic fillings for the pies. *Never underestimate novelty value,* he thought. He then began to wonder what Mrs Biggle may have tucked away in her cellar under the Post Office, so off they went to find pastry fillings for the discerning palette.

Chapter Eleven

Cuthbert stared; it was like the interior to Tutankhamen's tomb. When Percy asked what was in there, Cuthbert breathed, "Wonderful things, Percy, wonderful things."

Percy pushed forward and it was his turn to gape and stare. The shelves in Mrs Biggle's cellar were crammed with old toys. Everything you could mention. Clockwork train sets, dolls prams, brightly painted toy soldiers made from lead and fantastic tin-plate aeroplanes with spinning propellers.

Mrs Biggle looked slightly uncomfortable as Cuthbert gently touched toy after toy. "I never had anything like this," he breathed. "Why are they all down here?"

She coughed nervously. "Well, you see Mr Biggle rather liked his toys and when they were delivered, he couldn't bear to sell them, especially not to the local kids. Many's a time he would say to me, 'Can you imagine how that dopey kid from the farm would treat one of these'?"

Cuthbert shrieked, "That was me!" before he realised what he was admitting to.

"Oh!" said Mrs Biggle.

Percy patted his friend on the shoulder and went off in search of the exotic ingredient.

Mrs Biggle went back to tend to the Post Office and Cuthbert was alone with his reminiscences. Most of his toys had been made from left over pastry on baking day.

His mum once made him a full set of the twelve apostles. What he was supposed to do with twelve men all standing bolt upright with blurred faces, had always been a puzzle to Cuthbert. By the time a squirrel had attacked Simon, the labourer had trodden on Mark, and John and James had been left out in the rain, all Cuthbert could play at was a casualty clearing station.

The 'Noah's Ark' scene was even worse. Some of the creatures made 'The Island of Dr Moreau' look like Crufts.

That had been when Mr Biggle had called by with some letters and spotted Cuthbert 'neglecting' his toys.

Cuthbert looked enviously at the shelves of bright, shiny

childhood playthings. "Huh," he sneered, "a grown-up playing with toys." As he looked for Percy, he carefully checked the walls in case any of the tunnels under his house were linked to the Post Office.

Percy was lifting boxes of tins down and examining them. "What are 'Nuclear Emergency Rations'?" he asked.

Avril stared out at the street resentfully. Here she was, the only career woman in the Valley and no-one would take her seriously. She wouldn't be fooled by these 'country bumpkins' again. Even when that car screeched to a halt and two men got out wearing black suits and rubber masks yesterday.

Ronald was quite convincing when he started shooting back at them, but the one who was supposed to be wounded was pathetic. As for Ronald tying them up and putting them in the boot in broad daylight before driving off and walking back alone? *Please*! Who did they think they were dealing with?

Ronald even sidled into her office later and gave her a bottle of perfume with Chinese writing on before asking if anything interesting had happened today? Because she hadn't fallen for it.

There was a scoop out there somewhere and *she would find it*. She placed the perfume bottle on the desk and noticed how the bright sunlight made it bubble.

Ronald had been quite shaken by the incident with the assassins. His chequered past always had the potential for catching up with him, but the Valley seemed so divorced from reality that he actually felt safe here.

Re-arranging his demolitions kit and reloading his gun, he noticed a gap on the shelf. *Wasn't there a bottle of liquid explosive there this morning?*

Looking around his room, he spotted the bottle of expensive perfume he was supposed to bribe Avril with. *Oops,* he thought. He had sub-consciously followed procedure and tried to eliminate all witnesses. Avril had the bomb.

Avril checked her calendar. Today was the day the bus company sent a bus hurtling through the village without stopping, just to keep the contract for that route; she still hadn't solved the riddle of why someone threw sheepskins at it somewhere along its route. *Perhaps that might fill a page,* she mused and, picking up her notebook, she headed outside.

In the distance, she heard the old-fashioned bulb horn sound as the bus warned everyone of its approach.

Blind-Pugh sprang into action and rounded up his sheep, and Avril decided to try a splash of perfume. After all, she might be interviewing young bus drivers all day.

Turning back into her office, she was rudely knocked aside by Ronald heading for the street with a bottle in his hand.

Checking her desk, she thought, *Phew, at least he didn't knock my perfume over*, and struggled to undo the lid.

Ronald dashed outside and threw the bottle as far away as he could. It landed in front of the bus, just as the sheep were being driven across the road. The whole scene disappeared in a blinding flash!

"Damn this lid," muttered Avril, as behind her the bus weaved from side to side trying to shake off lamb ready-meals and sheepskin rug samples.

Ronald executed a parachute roll and came to his feet well clear.

The bus careened through the village and out of the other side just as Avril got the top off the bottle.

The sheep dog returned to his kennel and lay down again. Being Blind-Pugh he couldn't see anything to get excited about, so he went back to sleep.

Ronald went in to see Avril. "Sorry about that," he said. "We could have all gone for a burton that time."

Avril looked down her nose at him and sighed. "Thank you for the perfume," she said. "It's lovely; but knock it off with the practical jokes, will you? I did go to public school, you know!" She then flounced out fragrantly.

66

Chapter Twelve

Arkle sat alone in the bar. She had a suspicion that the two bottom-feeders from the farm had used her pastry mix and everyone was admiring it. This was the only non-masculine success she had ever had and it could open up a whole new world for her.

Yes, she loved horses, not that they were much of a challenge. Once she sat on one, it was pretty subdued already. The rest mostly involved steering.

But this could be her entry into the world of frocks and fragrances. Perhaps, she would be photographed on the red carpet now, instead of in the winner's enclosure.

Cuthbert and Percy sat at the table. They couldn't decide whether Arkle was a threat or not; she seemed to watch them very closely lately.

Percy piled tins into pyramids and tried to choose a new pie filling, when one of the goats clattered down stairs, looked around and clattered back up again.

Cuthbert shook his head. "If those things get any fatter, they won't get through their own tunnels."

Percy's eyes lit up. *Goat Pie?*

Ronald and the Captain jostled into Cuthbert's kitchen. They had been squabbling about some past battle in some past war where some chap had done something to another chap and changed the world as we know it.

"If that doesn't deserve a medal, I don't know what does," stated Ronald finally.

"Humph," replied the Captain "What about the chaps who kept him fed and gave him all that energy, eh! Where's their medal?"

They sat, still arguing. Ronald felt quite strongly about this. "They can hardly be awarded the 'golden spatula', can they? 'Hot fat' isn't mentioned on a purple heart citation, they are just a bunch of REMF'S!"

The Captain leaned away in shock. "Take that back, "he

demanded.

"No," said Ronald petulantly.

The Captain stared and rose to an occasion of honour. Looking around desperately, he spotted one of Elspeth's discarded rubber gloves. Snatching it up, he slapped Ronald around the face with a loud 'Smack'. Breathing heavily he officially announced, "I challenge you to a duel. Tomorrow at dawn- you will require a second."

Ronald casually waved a hand in acknowledgement and the Captain left.

"What's a second?" asked Percy.

"What's a REMF?" asked Cuthbert.

Ronald was really rather preoccupied with the attempt on his life. His death had been announced several times under various aliases and yet they had found him. What would happen if they tried again? What would happen if there were more of them? Worst of all; what would happen when Margery saw those bullet holes in the front of the Mandrake Arms?

Glancing up out of his reverie, Ronald was startled by Cuthbert and Percy; both sat close to him, both keen to hear answers to questions he had already forgotten. *Oh, good grief,* he thought, *it's like rattling a paper bag near a puppy compound.*

At that precise moment, Percy's tongue lolled out and the picture was complete.

Ronald took a deep breath. "I've always been a front-line fighter. The Captain seems to have been some kind of cook. Now, there has always been an unspoken agreement between the two specialities." He paused. "They make the food. We eat the food. We don't ask what's in it and they don't ask if we enjoyed it. That way, we all get along fine. If the conversation ever gets any deeper, it turns out that they really could have been in the SAS, you know. It was only my dedication to food that stopped me."

"What's a second?" asked Cuthbert eagerly.

"What's a REMF?" asked Percy. They had swapped questions in case the other one got a better answer.

Ronald sighed again. "Apparently he has just challenged me to a duel to the death and I will need someone to act as a 'second' to supervise the event."

"What's a REMF?" they chorused together.

Ronald looked from one to the other and replied, "Rear Echelon

68

Meat Fryer."

Cuthbert and Percy sat back to absorb all this.

"What happens if he kills you?" asked Percy.

Ronald answered sarcastically, "I float through the clouds, carried by teddy-bears to a land where carrots are outlawed."

Percy was impressed. "What do the teddy-bears eat then?"

"That's rabbits, Percy," snapped Cuthbert, showing both his knowledge of undertaking and farming.

Ronald looked at them both in turn. If the face was the window to the soul, these two had been boarded-up years ago. They had survived every disaster thrown at them and several murder attempts. He knew that for a fact, because he'd been the one trying to murder them, but here they sat, not a care in the world.

Unexpectedly, he felt safe here and began to relax. "Why did you ask us round anyway?" he asked.

Percy explained his need for a special pie and wondered if Ronald had come across anything different on his travels. Ronald leaned back in his chair and put his feet up on a strange lump under the table. "I've seen things you wouldn't believe," he began. "I have been in countries where they eat anything that flies except an aeroplane, and others where they eat anything with four legs that isn't a table. In one of the places I've been, the things on two legs weren't too safe either."

Ronald kept the two of them entertained all afternoon.

Percy made notes and listed 'Mongoose', 'Boa steaks' and 'Water off a duck's back' as of particular interest.

When Ronald prepared to leave, Cuthbert asked, "So what happens tomorrow at dawn then?"

Ronald paused for thought. "If I lose, there'll be another obituary I suppose ..." He brightened immediately. "Cuthbert, you're a genius! I will simply lose and be buried again." Nearly dislocating Cuthbert's shoulder with a playful thump, he added, "And you can arrange it all, mate," and then he left.

Cuthbert turned smugly to Percy and said, "I'm a genius."

Percy was too busy to be envious; he was carrying a bucket of water and looking for a duck.

Chapter Thirteen

Avril was annoyed. The burglar alarm had gone off at the office and it was the middle of the night.

The first time this had happened, it had been Percy wondering what it was and throwing a brick at it. The second time it had been Percy who had forgotten what happened every time he threw a brick at it.

Avril began to unlock the newspaper office door. She really was annoyed and when Avril was annoyed, well, watch out. She could easily push someone over! She entered the code and the irritating chirruping stopped. She sat in her chair for a moment. *It is almost dawn,* she thought, and then a sound caught her attention. It was the 'clack' of a pebble hitting a wall.

She darted outside, just as Percy picked up another pebble. "Morning, Percy," she trilled.

Percy was surprised to see anyone come out of the office at this time in a morning, but it was someone to talk to. "Morning!" he said cheerfully.

Avril stood right in front of him and asked sweetly, "Do you remember what happens when you throw one of those?"

Percy scratched his head and threw it just to check.

Avril kicked him on the shin.

"Ow!" said Percy.

"Let's re-cap, shall we?" asked Avril in the same sweet tone. "Throw," said Avril, and then kicked him.

"Ow!" said Percy.

"Throw," said Avril; then kicked him again.

"Ow!" said Percy again.

The sequence was repeated until Percy began to see that action plus pain equalled consequences.

Avril left him rubbing his shin. Having a little brother wasn't such a complete waste, after all.

Back in her chair, Avril raised the big green blind and stared down the street.

Cuthbert cut a sombre figure in his funeral clothing complete with top hat and ribbon. He walked slowly to the centre of the street and stood waiting.

From different ends of the street people began to appear.

Ronald and Henry walked slowly towards Cuthbert from one end.

The Captain and Percy came the other way. Percy seemed to be limping.

When they all met in the middle, Avril watched as Cuthbert produced two swords and offered them to Ronald and the Captain; both men shook their heads.

Cuthbert stuck the swords into the ground where they wobbled dramatically and produced two pistols. This time, the men accepted the weapons. Shrugging off their cloaks, they stood back to back and began to walk away from each other.

Avril almost collapsed with laughter. "Oh yes, right," she spluttered. "The first duel to the death in three hundred years and it's taking place right in front of me just after the alarm goes off. Really, they don't give up easily, do they?" She dropped the big green blind to show her contempt for their efforts and turned her back to the window.

The bullet came through the glass, through the green blind, whistled above her head and embedded itself in her one hundred yards swimming certificate. (The wall had looked rather bare without some of her early stuff.)

Grabbing her notebook and camera, she rushed outside and gasped.

Ronald lay flat on his back, his gun lying nearby.

The Captain had lowered his weapon and Cuthbert had removed his top hat.

"Oh, my goodness, oh, my goodness," repeated Avril, lifting her camera. "I missed it!" She looked imploringly at everyone present and asked, "Could we possibly do it again?"

The assassin perched on the hill watched the scene through his telescopic sight. It seemed that someone had saved him the trouble. His target was down. He would still claim the money though. Who would know any different?

Just then, he caught the flash of sunlight on glass. It was directly opposite his position. Checking carefully, he saw another sniper watching him. *It was a trap*, they both thought and, with only milliseconds to make a decision, both men fired.

Ronald, hearing the two shots almost simultaneously, sat up and said, "That went rather well," and Avril fainted.

Chapter Fourteen

Back at Cuthbert's kitchen, it was a celebratory atmosphere. Cuthbert and Ronald had checked for bodies on the hill sides, but a back-up team had removed all traces of anything.

"Hmm, professionals," noted Ronald appreciatively.

The women were roused, so that Avril would see a friendly face when she came round. She'd had enough shocks for one day.

Henry shook his head as he studied his brother. "What a strange world you inhabit," he said.

Ronald shrugged. "It's all relative," he replied. "You always looked suitably dramatic for your news broadcasts when you were nowhere near the action. Cuthbert is a fantastic chief mourner to a stranger when he really doesn't give a monkey's, and the Captain is a really good friend."

The Captain muttered suspiciously, "You do realise that I missed deliberately, don't you? It was all part of the plan."

Ronald grinned. "Yes, mate, the trouble was you also missed the newspaper office and I had to put one through the window for you."

Everyone laughed and silently toasted a scheme well carried out.

"What about me?" Percy asked hopefully.

Ronald paused, looked at Percy and said, "You, my old mate Percy," and he raised his cup in salute as Percy sat straighter, "convince me that there could be life on other planets."

Percy glared.

Arkle had saved a piece of the pie crust from when Constable Beeching demolished the 'bar snacks' and called the vet.

The poor man stood shaking before her wondering what horrors he faced this time. In a long and varied life, he had removed teeth from tigers and handled snakes having 'hissy-fits'. His arm seemed to have spent half of its life up some cow's bottom, but this woman terrified him.

He looked at the piece of pastry in amazement. "You want me to what?" he spluttered.

Arkle put her face closer to him in the time honoured way of the aristocracy speaking to the lower orders and barked, "Analyse it, man! I want to know what's in it."

The vet quaked. "Corned beef?" he tried in an attempt at humour. Arkle's expression never changed. He wasn't surprised; he had never tried to make granite laugh before.

Avril sipped her sweet tea. "They hate me," she sobbed, "just because I have a successful career and a bright future ahead of me."

Margery asked, "Why, giving up journalism, dear?" as she patted the girl's arm.

Avril straightened her back. "No, precisely the opposite," she said. "I am going to write an article that will expose them all." She counted off on her fingers. "We are harbouring a retired assassin. We have an undertaker who has no idea where people are buried or even who they were, and a gardener with so many multiple personalities he is his own family tree."

Margery grimaced and noticed that the other women were looking uncomfortable. "Now the problem with that, dear, is that you would also expose the rest of us. And besides, no-one would believe you; you don't even have a photo of the duel that didn't happen."

Avril slumped. "So what can I do to get revenge against these men?"

Margery perked up. She was on firm ground now. "Take every chance, dear, just like the rest of us. When you can poke, poke! When you can frustrate, frustrate! We slowly drive them mad. It's called 'the death of a thousand cuts'." Margery paused. "If you are really sadistic you can always throw in the occasional 'Don't you love me anymore?' That really keeps the wheels spinning."

Ronald, the Captain and Henry went off to compose a suitable obituary for the newly deceased and freshly resurrected Ronald, and Percy watched Cuthbert wash the cups.

When Cuthbert sat back down, Percy asked, "Quick, straight off the top of your head, what's the main thing to put in a pie?"

"Flour?" hazarded Cuthbert.

"Flower?" sneered Percy.

"Yes, flour!" said Cuthbert defensively.

Flower, mused Percy. Out came the grubby scrap of paper and the stubby pencil. Percy began to create. After a few lines he looked admiringly at Cuthbert. "Ronald was right, you *are* a genius," and he carried on writing as Cuthbert beamed.

Percy paused for a moment. "What do you call those people who won't eat something because they're deficient in something else?"

Cuthbert felt his new reputation slipping, "Idiots?" he tried.

Percy stared at him, obviously prepared to forgive a little flippancy, but not too much.

Cuthbert took a breath. "Oh! You mean protein deficient syndrome sufferers who fail to metabolise particles of indigestible matter?"

Percy stared again. "No, I meant vegetarians." Percy scribbled some more before adding, "Don't let this genius business go to your head, mate."

Cuthbert waited for the list to be finished and patiently waited some more whilst Percy tried to read his own writing.

Percy cleared his throat. "Right," he said, "vegetarians will give their eye-teeth for this lot."

"Do they have any?" asked Cuthbert.

"Do they have any what?" Percy enquired.

"Eye-teeth," said Cuthbert. "If they only eat grass and stuff, why would they need teeth?"

Percy asked, "Are you saying that vegetarians are born without teeth?"

Cuthbert sat back. "It would explain a lot," he said.

Percy tried sarcasm. "Do you think they come ready fitted with sandals then?"

Cuthbert thought, *they'd have to, I suppose, to stamp on the nuts.*

Percy slowly scanned his list. Somehow 'Daffodil fancies,' 'Tulip tart,' and 'Cactus surprise' had all the ingredients for a long afternoon with Cuthbert in this mood. Carefully folding the paper, he stood and headed for the door.

Cuthbert suddenly clicked his fingers. "I know," he said. "What was that meal fit for a King? Four and twenty blackbirds, wasn't it?"

Percy closed the door behind him. *Yeah, right,* he thought, *where am I going to get four and twenty blackbirds?* Just then, the crow sailed serenely overhead.

Chapter Fifteen

A Vet's waiting room is never a quiet or relaxing place. There is a statutory background noise of yapping, yelping and snuffling. Various owners are constantly chiding the animals, as if to convince others that their pet actually understands them.

The Vet sat in his little room enjoying the peace that would be shattered when he opened the door. He stretched, he yawned and he listened. It was silent. Had everyone gone home? Opening the door, he was greeted by an obstacle in tweed- he could smell horse.

Arkle barged in and the Vet glanced into the waiting room. Little red eyes peered from behind bars and dogs tried to burrow under the furniture.

The adults all had magazines held rigidly before them. *No help from that quarter then,* he thought.

Arkle perused the report from the Vet's analysis. "I already know all this," she snapped. "Hang on a minute, what's factor 'x'?"

The Vet shrugged. "We don't know; that's why we called it factor 'x'." He smirked slightly, but rapidly amended it to a nervous tic as Arkle turned on him.

"This pastry underwent a rapid, cataclysmic treatment and I need to know what it was. Where do I send it to next?"

The Vet quaked helplessly as he suggested, "A metallurgist?"

It wasn't often that the crow visited his relatives. They had all become city dwellers, content in their high-rise apartments; right at the top of the trees. Never a moment's peace. Cracking view though, he had to admit. At the moment, half of the rookery peered over the edge of its nests, watching 'the little scruffy one' creeping through the long grass towards them.

"Why does he think we can't see him from right up here?" asked an inquisitive chick.

The crow looked at it fondly and adopted the tone of a superior uncle from out of town. "Humans are strange things, young Joe Crow. They hide inside machines and then put windows in so that you can see them. They hide inside flying things that anyone can hear from miles away and when they want to be really sneaky, they put a fake duck on their heads and crawl through the long grass."

Joe Crow stretched his neck to watch Percy approach and asked, "So, out of all of nature, how come they rule the world?"

The crow stretched his wings and laughed. "Quite simple really," he said. "None of us wants it!"

Joe Crow continued to watch, as did half of the inhabitants who had the day off. The other half were down below, following the little scruffy one on foot through the long grass. From this height and to anyone with a crow's memory, it was Rorkes Drift all over again.

Percy advanced slowly into the clearing.

Cuthbert lay on his back fast asleep.

Percy gave him a kick. "Wake up, I've brought the net."

Cuthbert rolled over. "Do you think they've seen us?" he asked.

Percy snorted, "Probably seen you! You haven't made any attempt at camouflage."

They each grasped one side of the big net and fastened a stone to it.

Percy explained the plan once again. "When I send the hawk up and the crows flee in terror, we each fire a stone from a catapult. This will take the net into the air and catch four and twenty of them."

Cuthbert finished tying his stone and asked, "When you say *send* the hawk, do you mean *throw*?

Percy frowned at him. "All right, when I *throw* the hawk, if it makes you happy."

Cuthbert continued, "When you say throw the *hawk*, do you mean the *duck*?"

Percy glared and chewed his fingernail. "All right then, when I throw the duck. Is that better?"

Cuthbert persisted, "When you say duck, do you mean the *stuffed* duck?"

Percy whispered explosively, "All right, Cuthbert, when I throw the stuffed duck, we fire the net, got it?"

Cuthbert nodded.

Percy calmed his breathing. "Right then, on the count of three. One, two …"

"Caw!" interrupted his count.

He looked at Cuthbert in astonishment. "I said on the count of three; how did you reach *four*?"

Cuthbert raised his eyebrows. "It wasn't me."

They both looked around. "Ooh! Aren't they big close up?" said Cuthbert.

Percy fired his catapult.

Cuthbert didn't. The net wrapped around Cuthbert, until he was trussed like a turkey. They would soon have a whole bird sanctuary.

Percy fled one way with large crows demolishing the stuffed duck on his head and Cuthbert was left to roll downhill in the general direction of escape.

The crow watched from his vantage point and shook his head. *Such a poor species,* he thought. *I wonder if it's time for a cull?*

Swivelling Simon pushed his glass eye to one side in an attempt to focus on the objects on the table top.

One lung Louie tried to breathe and take in the aroma at the same time.

The drains inspector prodded the items suspiciously. "You actually *made* them?" he asked.

Buster shifted uncomfortably. "Well, you see, my mum really wanted a girl and she taught me all this stuff in case I changed my mind later on."

"Later on?" asked Simon, losing the battle to focus.

Buster stared at the floor and admitted, "Well, my uncle Harry(ette) always said he was uncomfortable in his body and one day he changed everything. Mum kept an eye on me, in case it was in my jeans."

Louie looked up. "You mean genes," he suggested.

Buster allowed, "She wasn't too comfy with herself either."

Simon had to ask. "When you say 'not comfortable', do you mean like itchy underpants, that sort of thing?"

"They wouldn't have helped," admitted Buster.

The drains inspector tried to get everyone's attention back to the table. It was like trying to paint numbers on escaping fleas.

"Well, these pasties look and smell delicious, Buster," he said. "Even the edges are crinkly, like the ones my mum used to make."

"Was she 'comfortable'?" asked Simon suspiciously.

78

"She most certainly was," snapped the affronted drains inspector. "And I only used dolls for throwing stones at!" he added defensively.

Each of them sampled Buster's meat pasties and the room settled into a hum of satisfied superlatives.

Chapter Sixteen

Ronald sat at Cuthbert's table with his feet up and watched as Percy staggered in. His hat was in tatters and feathers hung down dejectedly from what was left of it.

Ronald smirked. "White man has heap powerful medicine, eh, Percy?"

Percy scowled at him.

Cuthbert bumped into the doorway, trying to rock himself inside and was greeted with, "Fallen out with Spiderman, have we, Cuthbert?"

As the two began to tidy each other up, Ronald offered, "When I was a kid, we always agreed what we were playing before we started. That way, the knights of the round table didn't get annihilated by a plasma laser in the first few minutes."

Ronald was enjoying himself. Being dead had its advantages; whatever he was accused of he had the epitaph 'it wasn't me'.

Gradually piecing the tale together, Ronald became interested. Guerrilla warfare was his speciality and a campaign against the rookery would relieve some of the boredom of his recent demise.

He accepted a cup of indefinable liquid from Percy and they sketched out a map of the area. Ronald began a list of weaponry he might require. Anti-vehicle mines, anti-personnel mines, trip-wires, rocket launchers and chain-saws.

Henry entered and glanced over Ronald's shoulder. "Hmm," he noted, "anti-personnel mines for something that weighs as much as a bag of feathers, trip-wires for creatures that hardly ever land, and vehicle mines in case they try to escape by Skoda; you've thought of everything, Ronald."

Ronald sighed patiently at his brother. "This is the unrevised primary list."

Henry asked, "What if you can't get hold of the things on it?"

Ronald drew out another sheet of paper. "Then I compile a revised secondary list."

Henry persisted, "And if you can't get those things either?"

Ronald acknowledged the problem and nodded towards Percy. "Then I will be reduced to using a catapult and a net, like big chief running Plumm here."

Percy would normally have treated Ronald to one of his fiercest glares, but he seemed preoccupied. As everyone began to focus on him and silence descended, Percy shuffled and said quietly, "I can't understand it; we Plumms' have always had an almost telepathic understanding of birds. One of my ancestors could teach them anything; he even taught a matched pair of doves to sing, dance and even talk. He was so excited that he sent them ahead for Grandma Plumm's birthday by fast coach while he followed on horseback. All the way there, he was imagining the excitement after the months of work he put in. He burst into Grandma Plumm's cottage and spluttering with impatience, demanded to know what the old lady thought of the doves. Old Grandma Plumm looked up from her knitting and said, 'Oh, the birds, thank you so much, they were *delicious.*' My ancestor nearly fainted. 'You didn't eat them, Grandma? I spent months training them, they could sing, they could dance, they could even *TALK!*' Grandma Plumm simply sniffed and replied, 'Well, they should have said something then'."

The crow had been convinced into spending the night with his hosts; for a solitary bachelor bird, this was a major detour. By the time everyone in the rookery had wished everybody else goodnight, he should have been dreaming of all the great and good things which weren't available to him in his world.

Little Joe Crow had finally nodded off after that old crow next door started everybody off again by forgetting that she had started it all in the first place. At last, the crow could feel the gentle sway of the tree and the lulling whisper of the wind. A bit of stray feather stuck to his beak disturbed him and he leaned over the edge of the nest to shake it clear.

There were three of them this time, all wearing strange masks over their faces. He recognised the faint hum from the batteries of the night vision goggles with heat detection. Why did this species insist on taking part in things they were simply not equipped for? The crow balanced on the edge of the nest and swooped down in a silent spiral to land behind the three intrepid intruders.

Percy carefully scanned the ground behind them as Ronald had taught him.

Crows have a remarkably small heat signature, so all Percy saw were two green eyes looking back at him.

Quickly running through all the perceived threats Ronald had warned him about, Percy discounted this as two fire-flies holding hands and carried on sneaking forward.

The crow waddled along with him.

Ronald signalled behind him with a small torch. The original plan had been a series of finger-clicks, but Cuthbert couldn't line his fingers and thumbs up in daylight, never mind at night, so they resorted to short flashes.

Percy had a moment of suspicion. Ronald's torch beam was white, but the night vision goggles made everything green. So, if white was green, why were two white spots following him?

He swung around to check, just as the crow closed one eye to preserve his night vision.

Percy saw the one fire-fly and shook his head. *Relationships, eh,* he thought, *they never last*, and crept onwards.

Ronald gathered Cuthbert and Percy around him in the darkness and reminded them of the capabilities of the assault suits they were wearing.

By means of hand signals, the crow learnt that if he pulled the worm dangling from a top pocket, things would get brighter and if he pulled a worm dangling from a side pocket things could disappear altogether.

Noticing that a long stick emerged from Cuthbert's pocket, the crow helped it along and dropped it into Percy's welly. Way up above, the nests were silhouetted against the slightly lighter sky and the colony slept on.

Arkle paced her room; it may as well have been a tack room. The walls were hung with bridles and harnesses and there was an umbrella stand full of whips.

When a plumber came in to fix the radiator, he thought he had stumbled upon a bondage chamber and fled.

The only feminine touch was her pyjamas. Brightly coloured 'Thelwell' prints of oddly shaped girls on oddly shaped ponies galloped in all directions. Buying them in her size had been a problem, until the range was extended to include curtains. She had to find out what those two misfits did to her pastry.

Margery seemed to know her way around the tunnels, perhaps that was the answer.

With a wave of his hand, Ronald sent Cuthbert forward. It was his job to reach the foot of the trees unseen and begin to climb, using the hand-spikes. Then he could throw a whole nest down into Percy's net.

Ronald, meanwhile, would plant charges around the trunks of the other trees and bring down as many as possible.

The next wave of his hand sent Percy scurrying forward with the net. He didn't remember giving Percy all those explosives to tuck into his wellies, he thought as he watched him go past.

Scrambling forward himself, Ronald reached the base of a tree and reached into his pocket. The explosives had gone. Checking all his pockets gave him the same news. *Percy, you twit,* he thought. *He has got mixed up and thinks I've got the net.*

Cuthbert waited until Percy joined him and stabbed the spike into the tree trunk. It stuck! Pulling himself up, he jammed another into the wood and it stuck too. He climbed up, but found he couldn't free any of the spikes to use higher up.

Percy was getting confused. Cuthbert was above him saying, "I can't go up!" Ronald was behind him somewhere hissing, "I can't *blow* up!" Percy held the net thinking, *these wellies are getting tight.*

Ronald hissed, "Welly, in your welly!"

Cuthbert said from above, "He's asking if you're in your wellies."

Percy snorted, "Of course I am; what else would I wear?"

Ronald hissed again, "Percy, I need your welly."

Once again, Cuthbert translated from above. "Percy, he needs your welly."

"What for?" asked Percy in disbelief.

Cuthbert was getting fed up. "How do I know, I'm half-way up a tree."

Percy grumbled to himself and, dropping the net, slipped off a welly and lobbed it high in the air towards Ronald, not seeing the explosives spilling out in the dark.

The welly hit Ronald right on top of the head, but at least he had it. Fumbling in its murky depths, Ronald realised that it was empty. "No, the other one!" he hissed.

Percy lobbed the other one, sending more explosives scattering about in the dark. This one landed at Ronald's side and was also empty. "Damn and blast!" snarled Ronald as he slapped his hand against the tree trunk, forgetting that he had been holding the firing button.

The ripple of explosions leapt from Percy's end of the clearing to Ronald's in seconds, blowing Cuthbert off the tree, and sending them all scattering into the darkness.

The crow flapped upwards with a spare stick in its beak to reassure the rookery that all was well.

Accusations flew thick and fast around Cuthbert's table, but it was impossible to say what had happened. They calmed and sat in silence. "Can anyone smell horse?" asked Cuthbert.

Avril stared at the empty street. It reminded her of one of the ghost towns in the old movies where tumbleweed would come bowling along in the wind.

Probably mistake it for Percy, she thought with a giggle.

Pull yourself together, girl, she admonished herself. *That way lays madness, or worse, a lifetime in the Valley.*

She was still puzzled. Where was everybody, why didn't she see anyone?

Avril had a sudden suspicion that it was because she was looking for them. She began to pretend to work furiously at her desk, turning suddenly at random to catch someone sneaking about. After jerking her neck sharply several times, she developed a headache and stopped it. Then a thought crossed her mind, *the tunnels!* Did everyone use the tunnels because they knew she was watching?

She suddenly felt very lonely imagining the rest of the community busily travelling beneath her and passing the time of day unseen.

Perhaps there is a coffee shop. That was really depressing, thinking of all the relaxed gossip surrounded by soft furnishings and chrome.

Avril looked at her waste bin and the empty yoghurt carton gaped back at her.

Abruptly, in her fevered imagination, there was a city under the Valley. The tunnels were linked to other valleys and trains ran between

84

them; there was a theatre and the opera, people waved and called to each other.

A knock at the door startled her. A member of staff poked his head in and reminded her, "Save a whole page for tomorrows pumpkin carnival in the next valley, I'm going as a pumpkin."

The slate of fantasy was wiped clean by the blackboard rubber of reality as Avril made a note to get a pumpkin costume.

Arkle could see through a gap into Cuthbert's kitchen. The two twerps were there and so was Ronald. Scanning the room, she gasped; Ronald had his feet on her pastry cube! It looked very smooth on top, as if someone had been slicing it.

Feeling her way through the dark tunnel, Arkle's hand closed around what seemed to be a handle. It was ribbed to give a good grip.

This must be the way in, she thought, and twisted it.

The goat wasn't used to having its head wrenched around by the horn and being of a limited vocabulary, managed to lash out with all four feet at once.

Arkle bellowed in surprise, the goat bleated in pain and the three heroes all dived through the same window with a precision envied by the Red Arrows. Arkle eventually stumbled into the kitchen by thumping anything she could reach; she thumped opened a secret door, so she went through it.

The room had been cleared of its occupants, so she grabbed the pastry, hefted it onto her shoulder and left by the front door.

Cuthbert and Percy were hidden behind the stile and all they could see was a huge silhouette with a big square head leaving the building.

"What was that?" whispered Cuthbert.

"Dunno," said Percy, "but it had a right chip on its shoulder."

Avril wasn't a brave person at all. Her school had taught her to expect there would be a man somewhere at all times, so there was no point getting sweaty learning self-defence or anything.

She gripped her torch tightly and headed for the cemetery. It was the only place she could think of where the tunnels came out.

Heading uphill, she left the torch switched off to preserve her batteries and her night vision.

The article she wrote about girl guides had proven useful at last. Gradually, she could make out the shapes of headstones, so she kept to the path. Pausing to take a rest, Avril thought she could feel the ground shake slightly and that darker patch seemed to be getting nearer. There was a smell of horse.

Cuthbert was interested to know exactly what had been in his house. He just wasn't interested enough to find out.

Percy went all adventurous on him and somehow various strings from their assault suits became tangled, so where Percy went, Cuthbert followed.

The huge square-headed thing in front set a fast pace and Cuthbert struggled to keep up. It was only the threat of one of the strings pulling tight that kept him going at all. Ronald had packed the pockets and it could be attached to anything, from a grenade to an inflatable boat.

Percy signalled a halt and Cuthbert faithfully collided with him. This business of hand signals in the dark was beyond both of them.

Avril crouched behind a headstone and thought of the graveyard scene from Dickens where Pip met the convict. The only other graveyard scene she could remember was where hands came out of the earth and as her feet were sinking into soft soil, she concentrated on Pip.

Arkle set the pastry cube down for a moment. Percy gasped, "It has taken its head off!"

"Perhaps it's a helmet?" suggested Cuthbert.

Percy leapt to a conclusion. "Aliens!" he hissed. It had been aliens who had brought him to this Valley in the first place and he had never forgiven them for missing his ride. "Stand back," he whispered.

"I can't," whimpered Cuthbert.

"Why not?" asked Percy.

"Because we're tied together," he explained.

Percy took something from one of his pockets and unscrewed the top. "Oh, right," he mumbled. "This will be loud, cover my ears."

Cuthbert stared. "What about mine?" he asked.

Percy patiently explained he needed both hands to throw the

'flash-bang' and he didn't want to be deafened.

"Oh, fair enough," agreed Cuthbert, putting his hands over Percy's ears. Being this close to Percy, he risked being tickled by the rampant froth of red hair from under his cap, and Cuthbert's nose began to twitch.

Cuthbert sneezed, Percy threw, and Arkle had the pastry half-way back to her shoulder.

The 'flash-bang' landed in the crook of her arm and exploded, sending the pastry cube off into the night at high velocity.

Cuthbert and Percy watched each other with interest as their eardrums were sucked inside out and they could hear their own brains working.

Linking arms to keep the string slack, they fled downhill, away from the roaring behind them.

Reaching the farmhouse, they crashed into the kitchen to find Ronald at the table, and some recovery of their hearing.

"Quick," snapped Cuthbert, "we're tied together by these strings and could explode at any moment!"

Ronald wandered over and examined the situation. Seeing the tangled strings, he said, "Oh, sorry lads, I left the price tags on."

Avril recognised the shape before her; she wasn't a journalist for nothing! "Is that you, Ar …?"

The huge shadow replied, "Ar …?"

Avril quickly adapted. "*Ar*e you all right?"

Arkle loomed in front of her until Avril stood up to compensate. Arkle looked around. "Have you seen my pastry?" she asked.

Margery had known Elspeth for some time now and never ceased to wonder at her energy and drive. Even chatting over coffee, Elspeth dragged out the ironing board and worked as she talked. Even now, she was expounding on her theory for the evils of the world. "Take the Captain, for instance," she was saying, referring to her husband. "Left to himself, he would go through life without causing a ripple. And if he did, I would straighten it out behind him. If some of these figures from history had been properly looked after, they wouldn't have caused such mayhem."

Margery was intrigued. "How would that work, Elspeth?"

Elspeth considered for a moment as she folded, fluffed and stacked. "Well, that Genghis Khan for instance, can you imagine the state of his clothes? If he had come home to a nice hot bath and a freshly ironed shirt, perhaps he would have stayed in at night instead of going off ravaging and pillaging." Elspeth paused to sip her coffee before continuing. "Have you seen the uniforms that soldiers had to wear? Bright red coats, white trousers and shiny buttons! Only a man would design something like that and then tell them to roll around in the mud killing each other. No wonder they were in a bad mood when they met at Waterloo."

Margery rested her chin on her hand and listened in rapt attention. She thought the world had lost a gem when Elspeth decided to become a housewife.

Constable Beeching awoke with a start. Something had crashed through the roof of his cells and the place was full of dust. Peering in through the bars, he examined the meteorite. It wasn't glowing or anything, but it had obviously come a long way. He began rifling his drawers for the correct form. Was it vandalism or lost property?

Avril and Arkle walked back to the village together in the dark. Avril confided that she was lonely even amongst all these people. *"They always seemed to have something to do!"* she wailed.

Arkle looked at her strangely. "Hah! Rookie mistake," she barked. "Never try to make friends with people. They don't have the depth."

Avril stopped and stared. "Well, what else is there?"

"Animals," barked Arkle. "Always there, always hungry and always need to chew something; plenty of scope for a relationship there. They've never let *me* down."

Avril walked on dejectedly. *That's it then,* she thought, *I'll be known as the cat woman who used to be a reporter.*

The word reporter triggered something and Avril was moved to ask, "Why were you in the cemetery looking for pastry in the dark?"

Ronald was enjoying himself. He had emptied the pockets of Percy's assault vest and loudly speculated about what to put in them next time. "Bird-seed, obviously," he said. "If you feed them first, they might stop trying to eat *you*."

He pretended to tick off items on his fingers. "Lengths of elastic for retrieving wellies. We don't want a repeat of *that* rescue operation again, do we?" Clicking his fingers as if a sudden thought had occurred, he added, "Basic instruction book in sign language stating with 'breathe in, breathe out'."

Percy glowered silently from across the table. He still needed an exotic pie filling and a 'Ronald-burger' had sprung to mind.

Constable Beeching prodded the meteorite with a long stick.

He couldn't open the cell door because the key had been copied that many times, the lock was full of wax. He really should report it, but that usually brought attention to him. Every time someone remembered him, they delivered more forms for him to fill in.

This is probably a local matter, he thought, but how could he show he was taking care of things? Constable Beeching smiled. His training officer once commented that 'He was sure Beeching would bring something to the police service, but he wasn't sure what.'

Well, here it is, mister, thought the constable, writing out a sign on a piece of cardboard. Initiative was the constable's secret weapon. Others rarely witnessed it, because he was alone in this frontier outpost against the criminal hordes. Hanging the sign on the bars, he stood back and read out aloud, "Lost Property Office."

Chapter Seventeen

Avril and Arkle sat in a corner of the Mandrake Arms. They had agreed to begin a search for the pastry the next morning, and now, sitting together having a drink in the warmth they soon discovered they had absolutely nothing in common at all.

Constable Beeching squirmed through the doorway of the Mandrake Arms. He could never understand why old buildings had such narrow doorways. Didn't they have real men back then?

Checking the area for bar-snacks, he hid his disappointment, and watched as Henry poured him a pint. Henry adopted the tone of 'mine host' as he asked, "Anything new in the world of crime constable?"

Constable Beeching licked his lips as the pint glass frothed creamily before him. "Well," he replied, "there's this new taser weapon they've been trying out. It fires twenty thousand volts into the bad guys and makes them fall down instead of running away." He sipped his pint.

Henry raised an eyebrow. "How does it recognise the bad guys?"

The constable furrowed his brow. "They didn't explain that bit," he admitted. "Mind you, we've got some very clever men in the force, you know. Some of them know hundreds of crooks by name. They are called the 'filing squad.'"

Henry sighed. "Do you mean 'flying squad'?"

The constable thought and replied, "We've probably got one of those too for when the crooks try to go on holiday." Finishing his beer, he thanked Henry and added, "Well can't hang about, got a meteorite to guard."

Henry wished him goodnight and picked up the empty glass. The constable had paused in the doorway, and said, "It must be built into it."

Looking up, Henry asked, "What, built in to where?"

P.C, Beeching explained impatiently. "The taser, it must recognise the bad guys. When they tried it on me, I didn't feel a thing." He then left.

Henry looked around the bar, but it was one of those moments when no-one else was listening. *Being a landlord isn't all fun,* he thought.

Percy was searching the cemetery; it was no use finding the magic ingredient if there was no pastry to wrap it in.

Once they realised it had been Arkle in the dark last night, they checked under the table and discovered the pastry cube was missing. That explained the creature with the square head.

Stamping about and peering behind headstones, Percy couldn't figure out where it could have gone.

Picking up a large rock, he guessed where Arkle had been standing, simulated the 'boom' and threw the rock in the same direction. Hurtling amongst the gravestones, Percy weaved from side to side like a competitor in the slalom for wellies event.

The rock had curved gracefully and begun to descend. Striking a granite angel with a distinct 'clack,' it ricocheted from one headstone to another.

Percy ran on feeling like an accessory in a pinball game. Never taking his eyes from the flight of the rock, Percy headed downhill until his wellies came into contact with a grave covered in green ornamental gravel. Running like fury, Percy was getting nowhere as the gravel spat out behind him.

In the distance there was a tinkling sound and a voice shouted, "Oil!"

Percy stopped running; he knew the sound of trouble better than anyone. Hands in pockets and whistling nonchalantly, he wandered down to the police station where Constable Beeching stood looking at his beloved car.

"Morning, constable," said Percy cheerily. "Everything all right?"

Constable Beeching lifted his helmet and scratched his head. The blue light on top of his police car was smashed and shards of blue glass lay around him. "Don't really know," he said. "We seem to be on some sort of alien firing range. That's the second meteorite this week."

Percy surveyed the mess. "Pity you never married, mate," he offered. "She could have cleaned all this up for you."

Constable Beeching was watching the sky and answered absently. "Never bothered," he said. "Why give away half your food, just to get the other half cooked?"

Henry joined the regulars in the bar. Ronald seemed to be smiling at some private joke, Cuthbert looked around as if he had lost something and Percy was missing altogether.

As the village landlord, it fell to Henry to keep both the ale and the conversation flowing. Hoping for a bit of normality, he opened with, "You and Elspeth must have some amazing tales from your service days, Captain."

The Captain was always pleased to reminisce and the rest of the table would try to change the subject. That was the key to conversation in this place.

"Well, we did actually," began the Captain. "I remember dining with the local Maharaja once on his birthday. He only invited me, because Elspeth had been caught trying to dust his tigers. He asked me if she was a crackpot. Well, I thought he said '*crack shot*' and said 'yes, actually she is'. Seeing this as a chance to get back in favour, I sent a note to Elspeth explaining things. The meal went swimmingly, until Elspeth appeared with a rifle over her shoulder. Just as she entered the courtyard, the Maharaja's prize doves were released to celebrate his birthday and the old gal reacted instinctively, eight shots, eight doves. A personal best! She never did learn the local lingo, so she was quite flattered when the natives touched their foreheads and shouted 'crackpot' every time she went to the bazaar."

This seemed to be another example of 'landlord failure'. Henry sighed, sat back and joined the other waxworks around the table.

Constable Beeching looked around in surprise as Percy opened the police station door and entered. The constable always locked the door behind him in case anyone wanted to share his pizza. "How did you get in?" he demanded.

Percy waved a hand. "You let me in," he replied.

The officer paused. "Did I?" and then asked "When?"

Percy smiled. "Just after you said 'come in and look at my meteorite'."

The constable straightened. "No, I didn't, it's a secret."

"Well, how do I know about it then?"

Constable Beeching stared suspiciously at Percy. "Can you hear a humming noise?"

Percy didn't reply. It was impossible to talk and hum at the same

92

time. Percy continued to hum and nodded towards the 'meteorite' in the cell.

The officer's eyes widened. "Is it coming from there?" he asked, quaking slightly. "Should we run away?"

Percy nodded furiously, his lips were getting numb.

The constable had a revelation. "Perhaps the meteorite reacts when it senses one of its own is nearby." He looked at the 'rock' and then at Percy. The meteorite was still its old self, but Percy had gone quite purple from trying to keep the humming constant.

The constable yelled and cannoned into his desk. Rebounding, he bounced off the wall and eventually squeezed out of the door. Roaring away in his patrol car, he was furiously pushing at the button connected to the broken light that simply refused to flash.

Percy took a deep breath and his colour settled down again.

Henry tried Cuthbert. "Have you any interesting tales of undertaking in the Valley Cuthbert? Buried any famous people?"

"Not yet," replied Cuthbert, looking slyly at Ronald. "My Mum knew everyone, though. She would often say 'Cuthbert, tidy your room, what if Princess Margaret pops in'?"

The Captain spluttered. "Did she?"

Cuthbert looked at him. "Did she what?"

"Pop in!" asked the Captain in exasperation.

Cuthbert thought for a moment. "Don't know- I was always tidying my room."

Henry tried again. "Did she know anyone else famous then?"

Cuthbert held his hands up. "She knew *everybody*! Every time we met someone new, Mum would say 'I sat next to her at school'. It must have been somewhere else though; the village school only held six of us." Cuthbert paused and the occupants of the table waited. "Trouble was," began Cuthbert, "it wasn't much fun with her knowing everybody. Every time I did anything, somebody would say 'I know who you are, I'll tell your Mum'. But the really worrying one was when she said 'God will never forgive you, Cuthbert'. You don't come much better connected than that."

Henry looked around the table, opened his mouth in the direction of Ronald, changed his mind and went to clean some glasses.

93

Percy examined the lock on the cell door from all angles. Then he kicked the wall at a certain spot and the door swung open. The 'meteorite' looked familiar. Bouncing down the hill had rounded all the corners off, so that it didn't look like a cube anymore.

Quickly scribbling some 'hieroglyphs' on a piece of police stationery, he left it on the cell floor, closed the cell door behind him and walked away with his prize.

The desk sergeant in the next valley had quite forgotten they had anyone posted in Cuthbert's Valley. Now, looking at the heavily perspiring P.C. Beeching, he realised why he had forced himself to forget.

"Are you sure?" he asked for the umpteenth time.

Constable Beeching nodded vigorously.

The sergeant consulted the form in front of him. "A meteorite came through the roof of the police station and began humming?" He peered over the paper.

Beeching continued nodding.

"Suddenly a strange little chap with purple skin appeared behind you, after walking through the wall, and tried to rescue it?" Another glance followed with more nodding. "As you grappled with the alien, he took out 'some sort of ray-gun' and you went outside to protect the car?" Another look, another nod. "As you tried to drive away, the alien fired at you and disintegrated your blue-flashing light?" More glancing followed with more nodding. "Running out of petrol, you bravely went back for the spare can and discovered that the meteorite had gone and you found this note?"

The sergeant held up Percy's hastily scribbled message. Long slow look, rewarded by long slow nodding. The sergeant tried to ease the tension in the room by saying, "Pity they didn't write it on the back of a mars wrapper. We could have sent a car straight round."

P.C Beeching looked at him with open admiration and asked, "Is that forensics, Sarge?"

The sergeant gave Beeching a long hard stare. "You have to be very sure, Police Constable Beeching. I have sent this set of symbols to headquarters and it could involve some very strict enquiries from people we don't often hear about."

94

The machine in the corner began to clatter. The sergeant rose to his feet and tore off a sheet of paper. "Blooming heck!" he whispered.

When Cuthbert returned to his house, he found a triumphant Percy waiting for him. On the table was a vaguely round lump with several bent knives and forks lying about around it. Cuthbert stared. "Whistle sold you another cannon-ball?"

Percy huffed. "It's the pastry. I risked life and limb to get that back."

Cuthbert prodded the lump with a fork- it almost went 'clang'. "What's happened to it?" he asked.

Percy slumped. "I don't know. All the rolling about must have sent it hard, I can't make a dent in it."

Jasper sidled into the bar of the Mandrake Arms. He slid alongside Ronald and hissed, "Big black car, dark windows, two men."

Ronald palmed a ten pound note to Jasper and casually made for the gents.

One of the men in the doorway watched him go. The other man approached Henry and flipped open a leather wallet.

Henry had been a newscaster and war reporter, but even he raised an eyebrow. "Are you lost, gentlemen?" he asked politely.

The man had a face of granite; his expression never changed. "We search for the lost. We don't become them," he intoned seriously.

Someone the same height as Ronald came out of the gents and the other man stepped in front of him. "Where is the man who went in there?" asked a voice of gravel.

Ronald, with his coat turned inside out, cotton wool padding his cheeks and walking with a stoop, replied meekly, "Still in there mister, zip trouble I think"

The man barged past and Ronald left the building.

"What the devil's going on; who are you?" the Captain blustered.

The man at the bar simply asked, "Military man?"

Standing erect, the Captain snapped, "Most certainly."

The man looked him up and down and murmured, "Enjoy your retirement; there may not be much of it left."

Astonished, the Captain sat.

Marjorie, attracted by the change in attitude, joined Henry behind the bar.

The other man exited the gents with a furious expression and curtly shook his head. The one at the bar addressed them all. "We are here on government business. We have the highest clearance and we have the power to quarantine the Valley." He turned to Henry, who confirmed it.

"He's right; these are the men in black."

The first man asked in a low, deep voice, "Where would we find a certain Cuthbert?"

Cuthbert jumped as Marjorie appeared beside him. "Quick, whatever you're doing, stop doing it; lose it or get rid of it!"

As Cuthbert grappled with all those instructions and possibilities, Ronald burst in. "Quick, hide me. It's the men in black. Nobody's safe!"

Percy grabbed the pastry and shoved it into the oven, the door thudded shut.

The house door crashed open and two men stood inside flanking the exit. They both had their hands inside their coats.

One of the men spotted Ronald. "Weren't you in the pub just now?"

Ronald watched him defiantly. "That's my twin; he's got a drinking problem."

The other man looked at Marjorie. "Weren't *you* in the pub just now?"

Marjorie shrugged. "That was *my* twin; it's a Valley thing."

The men looked around. One of them produced a laminated piece of paper. He turned it towards them, so that they could see the hieroglyphs.

Percy sniggered.

"Anyone know what this is?" asked one of the men.

"Shopping list from Ventura six?" hazarded Ronald, relieved they were not after him. "Can't get Bovril out there for love or money," he quipped.

One of the men spoke quietly. "The obituary photo didn't do you justice."

Ronald shut up.

Marjorie crossed her arms. "Very sure of yourselves, aren't you? What do you want?"

The other man looked at her and said, "Heard there's quite an active Valley mafia in these parts; thought we might check their books."

Margery shut up. The man waited for a moment and then asked, "Any more questions?"

Percy looked them up and down from their black trilby hats, past their dark sunglasses, the black suits and on to the black shoes. "Why do they call you the men in black then?" he asked innocently.

The first man shut up.

The second man advanced slowly towards Percy. "Now, what do we have here?" he asked. "An enigma wrapped in a mystery perhaps? Or just a worm dressed as a gardener?"

Percy gulped.

The man continued around the table until he was opposite Cuthbert. He sat, and asked, "Do you know who we are?"

Cuthbert shook his head. Out of the enormous list of people he didn't know, hadn't known or had forgotten, these men were way down the list.

"We work for the Government. We investigate strange sightings. Some believe that the truth is out there." He nodded upwards. "We actually suspect that *the truth is in here*." He stabbed a finger onto the table top. He then held up the coded paper. "Perhaps you can translate this for us?"

Cuthbert squinted and adopted a beatific expression. It wasn't often that he held centre stage and he was going to enjoy this. He also used the face that appeared when he had accidentally embalmed himself. "When the co-ordinates line up, the result will be the answer to all the questions you have ever asked," he began.

The man swallowed hard and asked, "Who are you?"

Cuthbert smiled. "I am the link between this world and the next. I send those who qualify to the next level."

The man swallowed again and opened his mouth. A thud from upstairs interrupted him. He and his partner exchanged glances.

"Who is upstairs?" asked the man at the table, his hand sliding back under his jacket.

Cuthbert smiled and was silent; he had forgotten about the goats.

Another thud from another part of the house brought the man to

97

his feet. He looked slowly around the room assessing the threat. Another thud above him reminded him that it was upstairs. "I'm going in!" he said to his partner. "Radio check?"

The man at the door nodded and adjusted a curly wire running from his ear. "Black two, this is black one, are you receiving me?" asked the man whispering into his sleeve.

The man at the door raised his arm and whispered into his cuff, "Receiving you, black one, loud and clear, black two out."

Ronald observed dryly, "Gee, it must take years to learn *your* radio codes."

The two men in black nodded to each other and everyone watched as 'black one' began to climb the stairs. Soon he had disappeared and the journey was followed via the muted radio chatter. *"The whole upper storey is filled with some alien filling, tough yet crumbly. There are tunnels going in all directions and a strange smell."*

The man at the door whispered, *"Black two, do you think it's a hive?"*

There was silence for a moment. *"Black two, this is black one; affirmative, this is a hive. I am following a strong odour upwards through a recent tunnel. There are several dead ends, but there are sounds at the end of this one."*

The man at the door was sweating. *"If this is a hive, they will do all they can to protect it. Get out of there, black one, get out!"*

Reception suffered suddenly and a crackling came over the air. *"I see something (crackle), it's (crackle) awful. Those eyes (crackle) horns! Agggghhhh!"*

The man at the door was panicking. This was either a 'priority one, code red' or an 'immediate action code five'. If he let go of whatever was inside his coat to use his secure communications link, he would be defenceless and all the eyes in the room were on him. In desperation, he skidded his phone across the table where it stopped in front of Percy. "Quick, you! Call help."

Percy leaned towards the phone and without touching it, bawled "Help!" at the top of his voice. The man at the door stared; they were all staring back at him. And they were smiling again.

A clatter from the stairs distracted everyone as 'black one' fell head first into the room. They assumed it was 'black one' anyway. Even his partner had to admit, without the black hat, the shades and with his jacket eaten all the way up the back, he didn't look particularly menacing.

The man scrambled to his feet and lurched towards 'black two'. "Goats!" he shouted "Goats!"

'Black two' hesitated; if he forgot all these code words under pressure, perhaps he should take that school-crossing job after all.

Just then, the fattest goat he had ever seen clomped down the stairs and hauled itself into another tunnel, wearing a curly ear-piece. 'Black one 'slumped at the table, white skin and lack of equipment threatening both his authority and his dignity. He scowled at the people around the table and then addressed his colleague. "Do you smell a rat?"

The other man hesitated. "Actually, I smell horse."

The door slammed back flattening him against the wall and he slid down like a cartoon character.

Arkle stomped into the room and boomed, "Give it to me, Cuthbert; give it to me now!"

The 'man in black' felt terror for the first time in his life. Being one of the 'men in black' was a powerful thing, but being just a *man* in black' who had actually lost most of his 'black' surrounded by this bunch, simply wasn't covered in the manual. Wishing he was hiding behind his dark glasses, he surveyed the room.

Arkle blocked the doorway with her hands on her hips.

Ronald could smell weakness and slid his hand into his coat very deliberately.

Percy grinned at his own reflection in the back of a bent spoon.

Margery made a tiny nail file look menacing indeed and Cuthbert rolled his eyes upwards and beamed like a happy medium.

Writing furiously, the remaining 'man almost in black' said, "I think a clean bill of health for the Valley should do the trick."

A polite attempt to doff his hat to Arkle failed as his hand met thin air, so he just nodded as she stepped out of the doorway, and dragged his colleague out to the car.

After hearing a screeching U-turn, the occupants of Cuthbert's kitchen relaxed.

Technically, Arkle was still on the threshold, so she growled, "*Now*, Cuthbert!"

Cuthbert rolled his eyes back to where they should be and opened the oven door. Lifting out the smouldering 'meteorite,' he staggered over to the table and thumped it down.

"There you go Arr …!"

"Arr ...?" growled Arkle.

Cuthbert recovered. "Arrghh, it's hot!"

Arkle inspected the object. "That's not my pastry. My pastry was oven-shaped and golden. This is an old rock!"

The air suddenly filled with menace and the smell of a scorching table.

Cuthbert stammered an explanation that mainly implicated Percy, and Arkle turned her glare on him. Percy blamed Constable Beeching, and implied the original may have been eaten.

Arkle turned away, intent on finding both the truth and the pastry.

Margery spoke. "How did you know to come here, dear?"

Arkle turned and replied, "Henry shouted upstairs to tell me what was going on."

Percy saw his chance. "What exactly did he call you when he shouted upstairs?"

Arkle looked at him strangely before she replied, "*Daughter* of course, what did you expect?"

Percy shrugged and Arkle left.

Cuthbert picked up a small microphone that had fallen from the sleeve of 'black two' and whispered playfully, "Come in, black one, come, in black one" and grinned at everyone.

The goat peered around the end of a tunnel in his new shades and replied, "Ble-e-eaat!"

Constable Beeching tried to stand to attention, but it just made him rounder.

The man in black had finished swearing at him now and the other one was on a hard wooden bench groaned and tried to reconcile waking up in a provincial police station with their facilities paid for by a hidden budget labelled 'Extraordinary expenses, extraordinarily hard to explain'. It appeared that he, the aforementioned constable, was from an uncertain family background and his parents may not have been married.

Constable Beeching trusted that these were facts because these men were official, even though one of them had abandoned the dress code.

The desk sergeant had suffered too. After explaining he had simply followed official channels, he had been told that if he followed those channels again, he would see where all the other waste water with lumps in it ended up.

After the men left, the constable thought he should try to ease the tension a bit. "Phew," he began, "dealing with these city types is stressful, isn't it, Sarge?"

The Sergeant took a deep breath; he would need it for *his* exploration of the constable's family tree

Elspeth poured more mixture into the little cases and then added a swirl of chocolate to the top. It was quiet without Percy's company, but at least the crow nodded at all the right times.

She wasn't surprised when men were missing at vital moments. As a colonial army wife, she had just about faced it all. There was that time when the Captain had a bridge tournament in the next town just as the natives had revolted.

Elspeth had gathered all the wives and children under one roof and fought the attacking hordes off single handed. Dashing from window to window, she fired as the children reloaded for her. The women cleared up the empty cartridge cases so that 'There wouldn't be a mess to clear up later, dear.'

When the Captain came home and found all the ammunition gone, he accused the servants of stealing it. No wonder the natives saluted her in the bazaar and called her 'crack shot,' she thought.

Left alone, Cuthbert and Percy poked the pastry. A broken chain-saw in the corner was testament to its new durability and something had to be done. Percy had a head full of culinary challenges and no materials.

Cuthbert suddenly asked, "Wasn't it like this when it first came?"

Percy nodded sullenly.

Cuthbert persisted, "So what happened to change it?"

Percy glanced towards the cooking range and Cuthbert agreed. Perhaps a blast of heat would have the same effect again.

One complication was that Cuthbert, using his knowledge as an undertaker, had been basting the 'Rock' in embalming fluid for an hour on the premise that 'what didn't kill you, made you softer.'

Placing the dripping 'Rock' on the floor, they stood back and swung open the oven door. Even the oven gulped when it realised what it had done. The opportunistic flame shot out from its captivity and recreated the Northern Lights on a local level.

Too local for Cuthbert's taste.

The 'Rock' slumped into the shape of a mushroom top and the vapours sent the goats burrowing through the thatch to escape.

Elspeth entered and placed a tray of fresh baking on the table. 'The boys' seemed pre-occupied with whatever they were doing as they just stood there with black faces and big wide eyes. "Didn't mean to disturb you boys," she said. "I'll just leave this here for you, shall I?"

Cuthbert and Percy were still allowing the vapours to escape from their sinuses and the room to stop flashing, so they nodded.

Elspeth turned to leave when she spotted the mound of pastry on the floor. Scooping some up into her apron pocket, she asked. "Mind if I use some of yours, boys? I have a few more to make at home."

'The boys' nodded again and Elspeth left. Once she was home, the rolling out began.

Cuthbert's pastry certainly rolled out thinly, she acknowledged. Sometime later Elspeth took a break, made a cup of tea; she tried the new batch of pastry out herself and was really pleased with the result.

The Captain returned and glanced at his wife as he crossed the room. Then he glanced again. He stopped and had a proper look. "Good heavens, Elspeth," he said. "Have we still got that suit with all the buckles?"

Elspeth sighed as she stood. *Men,* she thought. The woman in the mirror sighed back at her. Elspeth stared, the woman stared back. Neither of them had a wrinkle between them!

Avril was writing furiously. *This was it,* she thought. *What a day,* she added. First a meteorite fell on the Valley, then 'The men in Black' came to investigate and, to top it all, Elspeth seemed to have invented an elixir of youth. They may have to award two Pulitzer prizes this year.

The bar at the Mandrake Arms was full. Only Cuthbert and Percy were missing. Avril's editor had visited and he saw her scribbling and came across. After a while, he laid his hand across her notebook and whispered, "We can't print that."

Avril was appalled. "Why not?" she shrieked.

The Editor confided, "The Men in Black do not exist. The meteorite does not exist and I have been warned that if we say anything, *we* will not exist."

Avril cursed under her breath and started another page.

Margery wandered behind her clearing tables and gasped, "You can't print that, dear."

Avril wailed, "Why ever not? It's the story of the decade."

Margery patted her shoulder gently. "Yes it is, dear, but look at it from our point of view. We're not all as young as you dear and everyone will assume we have been artificially helped. You wouldn't want to embarrass your friends, would you, dear?"

Avril used her intense vocabulary to argue the point inside her head, but it stayed inside her head and her hands began to crumple the page of her notebook.

"Thank you, dear," whispered Margery as she walked away.

Avril wondered whether her parents still had the ant farm from her old bedroom. That had seemed really complicated until she came out into the big wide world and now seemed to be simplicity itself after the Valley.

Cuthbert and Percy had lifted the pastry off the floor and onto the table in a show of hygiene awareness.

Percy had sliced a piece off and rolled it around a banana and this steamed in the oven as he prepared more experiments.

The tests bothered Cuthbert. Not only because some of them must be outlawed somewhere in the world, but also the fact that the pastry would not last forever. It was time to try to talk some sense into Percy.

Some sentences are really doom-laden, aren't they?

Percy was wrapping a sheet of pastry around a turnip when Cuthbert tried his hand at diplomacy. "Stop wasting pastry, Percy," was his opening gambit.

Percy paused and looked up at him with a cute smudge of flour on his nose. "If you've got something to say, just say it!" he said.

Cuthbert tried again. "Stop wasting pastry, Percy!" he repeated.

Percy narrowed his eyes. "We've known each other a long time, Cuthbert. Don't beat about the bush. Come straight out with it."

Cuthbert tried to rearrange the words. There were only four of them and they came out as "Stop wasting pastry, Percy."

Percy sighed dramatically and, dusting off his hands, moaned, "I can't concentrate with you hinting all over the place, Cuthbert. As soon as my 'Melon and Beef Medley' is ready, I'm going to take a break."

Cuthbert gave up and walked to the window. He stared out despondently.

"Are they still there?" asked Percy.

Cuthbert confirmed the truth. "Yes, they're queuing right down to the farm gate now."

They had been under siege ever since the news got out.

Cuthbert had never seen so many wrinkly women. They looked like rejects from a candle factory.

He turned to Percy who was trying to wrap a chicken in a pastry strait-jacket. "I'll have to use the tunnels to get supplies if this keeps up."

Cuthbert jumped as a voice close to his ear said, "Don't worry, boys, we've thought of that." He turned; the kitchen was full of women! Baskets and boxes were being stacked on the table allowing Percy's chicken to escape with a piece of his nose in its beak wearing a pastry waistcoat.

Margery patted Cuthbert on the shoulder and said, "We knew you would both be busy, so we bought some necessities for you."

Cuthbert noticed a panel in his wall sliding shut behind them.

Margery saw his glance and said, "You wouldn't make your friends queue up outside, would you, dear?"

Cuthbert and Percy instinctively stood close as the women emptied bag after bag onto the table.

"Disinfectant and dusters," announced Elspeth.

"Fresh air spray and deodorant," trilled Margery.

"Dried flowers and scented drawer liners," added Avril.

"Organic tofu!" squealed Geraldine.

Cuthbert leaned towards Percy and repeated, "I'll have to use the tunnels to get supplies if this keeps up!" He sidled away from Percy and eased himself towards the cellar entrance.

Percy had been distracted by the concept of 'Charcoal welly insoles' and was being bombarded with questions. "Where is your cleaning cupboard?" "Where is your fridge?" and the really frightening, "They must come off *some time,* Percy!"

Cuthbert giggled as he crept down the cellar steps. It wasn't often that Percy was left to face the music. He walked through the cellar

104

accompanied by the smell of apples and stepped into the tunnels to the smell of fresh air. He turned a corner and noticed *the smell of horse*.

The women outside were of a very patient variety. After all, hadn't they spent years cultivating these wrinkles?

The chance of re-birth was too good to miss. Each of them carried a mental image of the man they would spend the rest of their lives with. Oddly enough, it was never the man they were going home to.

One of the women asked, "Who is this Cuthbert anyway?"

Someone offered, "Local undertaker, bit of a weirdo"

The queue fell silent. Someone asked "What if it's a trick to get rid of us. What if we have been lured here for nefarious purposes?"

The women considered this. There was still time to escape. They could simply leave the queue and walk away exactly as they had arrived. On the other hand, they could face 'A fate worse than death' wrinkle free! Nobody moved.

Cuthbert didn't move either. One, he was terrified and two, Arkle wouldn't let him. "Where's my pastry, Cuthbert?" she hissed.

Cuthbert stammered out the story whilst Arkle patiently crushed his shoulder.

"So," Arkle concluded, "you can't operate without my pastry and I can't operate without your heat treatment and secret ingredient?"

Cuthbert nodded his head. It was the only bit that wasn't paralysed.

Arkle released him and offered her hand.

Cuthbert used one hand to lift the other one up and Arkle promptly shook all his bones back into place again.

"Partners then?" she boomed.

Cuthbert summoned up a sickly smile.

The woman standing roughly number ten in the queue said loudly, "You know, I can't see where the women before me need any treatment, can you, ladies? They must all be in their twenties."

The women at the front preened. The anonymous woman continued, "If I had their looks I would be applying for the job of

105

beautician advertised in the high street instead of being stuck here."

Several at the front of the queue shifted from one foot to another and suddenly one of them pretended to receive a phone call. "Must go," she said sheepishly. "Emergency."

Another one, seeing this as a ploy, followed closely, and her friend went with them.

Not bad, thought the woman, *now I'm seventh.*

Police Constable Beeching gasped with relief. The fall hadn't really hurt because he was well padded, but he had been stranded on the coat hooks for ages. He was only freed when part of the wall collapsed.

He stood and supported himself on the ominously groaning desk. He had a report to write; an assault on a police officer was a serious thing. Collecting his thoughts, he tried to arrange the sequence of events. He had entered the police station with a fresh pizza or two and had noticed a strange animal type smell, then something huge with freakish strength had picked him up, shaken him and demanded pastry. After he mentioned Cuthbert, the creature hung him up, stole his pizzas and left.

The constable tapped a pencil against his teeth and pondered a point. Was it more professional to refer to it as a 'Yeti' or 'Bigfoot' in his report?

Cuthbert retreated to his kitchen, only to find a stunned Percy sat staring into space. Cuthbert passed through several 'aroma zones' on his way across the room. One part smelled of 'Lilies of the Valley', another was 'citrus' and Percy seemed to be 'Peach Blossom'.

Cuthbert sat and asked, "What happened?" while looking around at the floral curtains and gleaming surfaces. The scrubbed table top defied him to lean on it.

"Apparently, we're all partners," murmured Percy. "The women will 'take us in hand' and 'show us the ropes' and if we argue they will beat us up."

Why was being a man such a challenge to women? Cuthbert thought.

106

Arkle pounded the pastry with her fists, flipped it into the air and pummelled it some more. *This is it,* she thought. *Supply the pastry until you work out the secret ingredient. Watch how they heat treat it and set up on your own.* She smiled grimly as the mixture came to heel and squashed its molecules together in desperation. She would have her own range, her own, named product. Her name would be up in lights. She paused and the pastry briefly considered fighting back, but a realisation made her thump it even harder. "Name in lights," she muttered. "What *is* my name?"

The queue outside was getting restless. The women from the other Valley had television. A woman's voice said, "I can't believe what is going to happen to Mildred in 'East-Valley Enders' tonight. After all these years as a favourite!" Tremors ran up and down the queue. The woman turned the screw. "And with *him*, of all people!" The queue began to disintegrate, lots of people left from behind her, but more importantly, three more went from in front. *Now she was fourth.*

Cuthbert opened another drawer in despair. It should have been full of tangled-up old shoe laces, but now it had scented paper and *kitchen implements.* His tool drawer was unrecognisable. The bent spoons and untwisted corkscrew were gone. All the bent nails and old screws had been cleared out and *something* was missing from the old tobacco tin. He couldn't remember what it was, but his dad had put it in there to keep it safe years ago.

The woman who was third in line was becoming irritated. The woman behind her was sneezing on the back of her neck. When she turned to complain, the woman behind was apologetic. Apparently, she had been abroad and brought something strange back with her. Even her cat had died. Women number two and three fled! *She was second now.*

The smell of peach blossom seemed to be following Percy about and he wasn't his old self at all. The fact he didn't even *smell* like Percy, only added to the confusion.

107

Cuthbert eventually discovered that Percy had been given a 'make-over'. His wellies had been forcibly removed and charcoal inserts placed inside and his pockets were full of devices that squirted perfume every time he moved. With his natural scent gone, he was like an actor looking for a character to fit into.

The woman at the front of the queue was not a vain person. She knew she wasn't, because she said so herself. She only waited to try this miracle product in the hope she could pioneer it for the rest of the world to benefit from. She really was a good person, she told herself.

At that moment, the farmhouse door opened. Everyone tensed and then relaxed as a scruffy little chap came out in turned down wellies. His pockets seemed to give off a puff of smoke every time he moved.

The woman behind the first in line leant forward and whispered, "That's the chap they test it on. Such a shame, he was a good looking guy when he went in."

The woman at the head of the queue analysed her pioneering spirit and realised she had left the gas on.

Now she was first.

Cuthbert wasn't really comfortable with chintz. He didn't even know what chintz was, but he didn't like being surrounded by it, so he went to look for Percy. As he left the front door someone at the head of the queue ran towards him shouting, "I'm first, I'm first!"

He pulled his thoughts together and said, "Oh, I'm sorry, the women took the new batch through the tunnels. They've been handing it out at the Post Office for hours. You had best get back there, Mrs Biggle."

Margery had been selling the pastry in cubes all day. There seemed no end to the customers.

Even Mrs Biggle turned up moaning about queuing up somewhere for something or other.

People were actually going away scratching their heads and wondering how to apply a cube when a scream from the street solved everyone's problem.

108

A woman with a completely blank face and her hands held out in front of her entered the shop and everyone ran away in terror. The newcomer looked familiar as she bumped into the crisp display and rebounded against the counter.

"Is that you, Elspeth?" asked Marjorie.

The blank faced woman faced the sound, nodded and mumbled, "I've got it, Marjorie. We roll it out very thin and use it as a face-mask."

Marjorie was impressed. "Excellent dear, do you think we should poke eye-holes in it too?"

Marvin read the sheet of paper again and called the road gang over to his desk. "Something's happening in the Valley," he said. "This is the latest analysis of the drains water; it seems it contains lumps of pastry and embalming fluid. Any ideas anyone?"

Simon swivelled helplessly in case they sent him to investigate.

Buster shrugged and Louie practiced his breathing techniques.

The drains inspector offered a little quip, "Sounds like the farm to me. Cuthbert's an undertaker and Percy's half-baked."

Marvin smiled dutifully. "But why is it ending up in the drains? We have full investigative powers, you know." His phone jangled and he picked it up absently. The second he heard the voice, Marvin shot to attention.

The drains inspector ushered 'the lads' out and mouthed a question, "The mayor?"

Marvin clenched his fists and his mouth stretched unnaturally. "Doreeen!" he mouthed back. The drains inspector paled. After putting down the phone, Marvin confided in the other man. "This is strange." He clenched his fists and grimaced. "Doreeen! has heard there is a miracle anti-wrinkle cream on sale in the Valley and she wants some."

The drains inspector said casually, "If it's that good, it'll be on sale everywhere soon."

Marvin looked at him pityingly and said. "You don't understand; she wants it *now*."

The road gang grumbled through the procedure as they filled the van with all the requisite tea-making gear and the odd tool in case they actually did anything. "How come this is so urgent?" asked Louie suspiciously.

"Where's the job sheet?" asked Simon equally suspiciously.

"Where's the van?" asked Buster.

After arguing with the accounts department that pack-mules had been replaced long ago and yes, they did need a van, it was returned to them. The lady delivering sandwiches complained about the smell in the back anyway.

Entering the Valley was always an ordeal for strangers. It was even worse for people who knew exactly what *could* happen here.

The road gang tried to get through the high street as fast as possible and reach the farm. The fewer natives they met on the way the better.

Buster gabbled something just as they rounded a corner near the Post Office and he almost ploughed into a crowd of faceless women. Shrieking even louder than the tyres, Buster avoided them all, but lost his argument with the horse trough.

The van tipped over on its side and screeched along the road losing all liquid content into a nearby drain.

"Marvellous!" said an upside down drains inspector. "The next drains analysis will show three months' supply of tea-bags and forty gallons of petrol."

Arkle was taking the next batch of pastry over to Cuthbert's. She amused herself by throwing it in front of her and then picking it up again. On her way through the village, she casually righted a council van full of grateful men and then she spotted the mass of women wearing pastry masks and giggled. She really must get these feminine ninnies riding or shooting or arm-wrestling pigs before they became a complete embarrassment.

Because Henry was organising a cricket match soon and she was the secret weapon, Arkle began practicing her bowling. She hurled the pastry cube ahead of her in the direction of Cuthbert's farm. She would pick it up later on the way over. Then she headed towards the group of women to investigate this new fashion statement.

Percy had just stepped over the stile and still had one welly in mid-air when a whistling sound distracted him.

The cube of pastry bounced and lifted him off his feet and he was propelled forward, sitting on a sliding cube.

Cuthbert came out of his door to look for Arkle, just as Percy skidded to a halt in front of him. Percy grinned. Cuthbert shook his head and said, "It'll never catch on."

The road gang cowered in the back of the van. The back doors were flapping open and they could see a horde of faceless women waiting to ambush them.

Swivelling Simon's eye had looked like the moon orbiting the earth when he saw Arkle approach. He thought she was going to finish them off. When they all fell on top of each other as some powerful force righted the van, the drains inspector could only manage a weak, "Thank you."

After untangling themselves, the team huddled together and watched as the crowd of women performed some strange ritual that involved bumping into each other until someone poked them in the eyes.

"Is that what we've been sent to fetch?" asked Buster pointing to the masks.

"I think so," admitted the drains inspector. "But we have to convince them that this is official and we need it for analysis."

Everyone seemed to stare at Buster. "Off you go then, lad," said the drains inspector.

"Where?" asked Buster.

"To convince them that this is official and we need it for analysis."

Buster left the van reluctantly and rehearsed his speech all the way across the road. It was eventually delivered as, "I am an official and I need one for my sis!"

Margery was not impressed. "If your sister wants one, she can queue up like everyone else. What do you say, girls?"

Buster gulped as the faceless women converged on him.

Cuthbert dragged the cube into his kitchen and with Percy's help they laid it into a deep bowl of embalming fluid. "Let's get this soaked before Arkle shows up," he said. "This is our secret."

They emptied two more bottles on top of the pastry and Percy exclaimed, "Just in time, mate, here she is."

The house shook twice as Arkle missed the door. She lifted her mask slightly and came in on the third attempt. "Oh! You found it," she said.

Cuthbert nodded. "Percy rode in on it."

Arkle removed the mask and put it in her pocket. She examined the bowl of liquid rather too keenly for Cuthbert's liking. "Is that the secret formula?" she asked directly.

Cuthbert gave a false laugh. "Oh, good heavens, no. It's ... what is it, Percy?" he asked desperately.

Percy answered calmly, "That's home-made wine, that is. Cuthbert likes a tipple." He mimed lifting a glass and staggered slightly.

Arkle sniffed at the fumes and picked up an empty bottle. "Embalming fluid?" she asked in horror, reading the label.

"Oh no!" cried Cuthbert. "We, er, we use the empty bottles, waste not want not."

Arkle remained suspicious. "So what is my pastry doing in it then?"

"Accident," said Percy. "Throwing it to one another and it slipped."

Cuthbert nodded in admiring agreement.

Arkle looked from one to the other.

Percy sighed. "All right, you've got us, but we were going to tell you if the experiment worked." Cuthbert adopted his 'waxwork under pressure' expression and waited for whatever fate may bring as Percy explained, "We thought that our home-made wine and your pastry might make a nice sherry trifle."

The tension in the room lessened somewhat as Arkle raised an eyebrow admiringly. Stooping, she scooped up a handful of liquid and held it under her nose.

Percy panicked and ran for the door, nudging Arkle's elbow as he went. The handful of embalming fluid went straight down her throat.

"Good grief," she spluttered, "I've tasted better worm medicine, Cuthbert."

Cuthbert's eyes widened. "I'll take your word for that," he muttered.

When Arkle left a few minutes later, Percy was hiding behind a stone wall and peeping through the gap. She seemed to have trouble steering herself! She tugged one sleeve down and it sent her one way and if she tugged on the other she went that way instead. Her teeth seemed to have slipped to the back of her mouth and she was desperately working her jaw to move them back. Each leg seemed to have a different ambition and she was lurching sideways most of the time.

Percy watched as she staggered down the track and he breathed a sigh of relief.

Buster was now surrounded by blank-faced women with outstretched arms and they were closing in.

Margery took pity on him and opened the flap in the counter. "Come on, escape out of the back door," she smiled.

Buster rushed past gratefully and managed to grab a spare mask as he went out.

The drains inspector saw him coming and slid into the driving seat. Turning the key, he stared in disbelief as the engine groaned and stopped. Buster dived into the back of the van and shouted, "Go! Go! Go! They're right behind me."

One lung Louie stammered, "Hurr, hurr, that big one is coming back too and she looks even stranger than when she went, hurr."

The drains inspector tore a bundle of wires out from under the dashboard and pressed the ends together. Sparks flew and the radio came on. He tried again and the wipers waved to him. "Run, lads, run for your lives," he yelled, jumping out of the van.

As they ran, Simon panted, "Why do we ever bring a van? We never take it back with us." One of his eyes watched the road ahead and the other one checked the sky.

Avril sat with her back to the street. There had been some commotion, as if a van had crashed and then frantic foot-falls as if several men were being chased by zombies. As if she was going to fall for that. She submitted to a moment of curiosity and glanced around.

Arkle lurched across into the middle of the road and back again making vague arm movements and clutching her throat.

"They're all at it now," Avril muttered. The blank page stared accusingly at her as she planned the day's headline. How would she ever create a sensation when they stopped all her stories at source?

She stared at the wall. Right next to her swimming certificate with a bullet hole in it, was a picture of her inspiration, Albert Einstein. At least he would never fail her. For a moment she had a horrible thought. At this angle, in this light, he looked like … Percy without his hat. That was a thought destined to remain buried deep.

Shuddering, she contemplated the typewriter. It sat smugly in front of the state of the art word processor. A device so packed with sophisticated gizmos that everything else would soon be redundant. Unfortunately, the stupid thing required electricity and some idiot had bought it for the Valley.

Avril gave another one of her 'frustrated reporter' sighs and thought, There's only one thing left. *Try to make the cake competition sound as exciting as the Olympics.*

Ignoring the modern plastic machine, April spun her chair towards the old typewriter left by her predecessor. The black and gold iron relic before her clattered into life, as she committed the Valley to a cut-throat, blood-curdling ordeal of mixing bowls and wooden spoons at dawn. Avril examined the finished article. Was this really her journalistic future? Would there ever be a light at the end of the tunnel? She sat up. Her brain was pointing her towards something; it may not be a light but it was definitely a glimmer of mischief. She headed towards the archives.

Margery scanned the front page of the local newspaper and Avril scanned the faces around her. It was traditional to show the new edition to the women's coffee morning in the Mandrake Arms before circulation. Basically it gave them time to issue a denial in case anything slipped through.

"Y-e-s," said Margery slowly, "very nice, dear. But you've rather committed us. We haven't even sorted out who will submit what in each category, you know."

Avril gazed around innocently and said, "Oh, sorry. I thought decisions were made and all the tarts lined up for it."

The women looked at her suspiciously. Could they scent rebellion?

Avril watched them in turn.

Elspeth had been the undisputed pastry queen until Cuthbert produced his wonder mix. Margery could turn her hand to anything. She could twist everyone else's *arm* too. You only had to watch Belinda being a barmaid for a moment and there were no further surprises there. Geraldine could bake when she wasn't digging up old graves, but tended to use the same tools and most people preferred their cakes without bits of other people in them! Arkle, well, Arkle meant well, but her last lot of cakes were still at the stables being used for mounting blocks. Mrs Biggle tended to use whatever ingredients she was stuck with and dried egg patties were an acquired taste.

Avril basked in the sunshine of a subtle revenge.

"Well then," said Margery, "we had better get prepared now that we are committed." She consulted the front page again. "'Trouncing the non-traditionalist usurpers for the crown of cooking-dom', unquote," she added to put the blame for atrocious prose firmly on Avril's shoulders. Rubbing her hands together, Margery began to ask for each of the women to offer their speciality ready for a 'cook-off' to decide the finalist.

"*Actually,*" said Avril deliberately, "after checking the rules, I have some rather startling news."

Geraldine tittered, "That's a first for the Triple Echo."

Avril waited for the smirks to be brought under control and savoured the moment. "The competition is only open to beginners!" she stated flatly.

The women all spoke at once. "That's me," "Just a housewife," and the favourite, "I've always been new at this."

Margery held up her hands. "It's all right, dears, I'm sure we all qualify."

"*Actually,*" began Avril, enjoying the effect that one word had on a group of conscience-stricken women. "According to the records, Margery, you have provided scones and various other items for the school fete for many years."

Margery snapped, "That was for charity."

Avril paused before replying. "I checked that too. The *Valley mafia* isn't registered as a charity."

Margery sat quietly.

115

Elspeth rose to the occasion. "Don't worry, girls, my oven is always on pre-heat and ready to go."

Avril dropped the dreaded word into the pond and watched the ripples spread. "*Actually*," she said, "there was the chapatti contest on the North West Frontier some years back and you did provide the catering for the golf tournament."

Elspeth sat, stricken.

Arkle stood. "About time! I'll step into the breach this time, girls. My time has come."

"*Actually*," began Avril, "you were caught at a gymkhana tenderising beef burgers by putting them under your saddle before the jump-offs!" Arkle sat.

Geraldine looked around reluctantly and offered, "Well, I will do my best of course, girls."

"*Actually*!" Avril rolled the word off her tongue. "There was that scandal on the last dig when some students slipped a mummy onto the barbecue." Geraldine deflated.

Mrs Biggle admitted defeat before anyone spoke. Thanks to phoning recipe hot-lines on her mobile whilst mixing, and blowing powder from her face powder compact, all her baking tasted of 'Passionate Mist'.

All eyes swivelled to Belinda. She beamed; she had always felt slightly inferior and now she could save the day.

"*Actually*," supplied Avril, right on cue, "there is the matter of the hot bar pasties."

Margery gasped, "Oh, good heavens, woman, she uses a microwave!"

Avril smiled. "But the newspaper has a photo of her *doing* it."

The women sat and seethed. Belinda sobbed. It was so unfair. She made cold snacks all year round and if the electricity suddenly came on everyone flocked to the bar for a hot one.

Margery took control. "All right, then *Actually-Avril,* who does qualify?"

Avril enjoyed the attention until the stares were analysed and they were *actually* rather hostile. She gulped. "Cuthbert, *actually*!" she gasped. So did everyone else.

"What the devil are you doing?" asked Cuthbert.

116

Percy was putting the finishing touches to a sculpture of Beethoven. He had the pastry on the table and it was so malleable that even the pointed collars and individual hairs could be shown.

Cuthbert scowled at it and Beethoven scowled back. "Why him?" asked Cuthbert.

Percy paused from his work and replied, "One of my ancestors owes him a lot." Smoothing the forehead, he continued, "My ancestor used to tune his piano for him; it earned him a nice living later."

Cuthbert was amazed, "I thought Beethoven was stone deaf?"

"He was!" and Percy adjusted the nose.

"Huh, good job your ancestor was a piano tuner then, Percy."

Percy looked up. "Oh, he wasn't, he was the gardener. They had trouble finding a good one; in fact my ancestor was the fifth. Beethoven did some of his best work after he'd fiddled with the keys for him."

The road gang burst into Cuthbert's kitchen and threw themselves into the chairs around the huge oak table. Cuthbert automatically set out the cups and started pouring the tea and Percy studied the exhausted faces and waited for an opportunity.

"Faceless women," gasped the drains inspector, "surrounded the van and tipped it over, had to run for our lives."

"I only just escaped with this," said Buster, carefully spreading the pastry mask out on the table.

Cuthbert explained the circumstances of the cooking competition and the unforeseen benefits of the pastry and the assembled workmen stared at the mask as each of them assessed its potential.

Percy broke into everyone's thoughts with, "One of my ancestors belonged to you lot, you know."

Every pair of eyes and one of Simon's swivelled across to focus on him. Percy shuffled and Cuthbert eased himself into another room.

"Oh yes," began Percy, "as the world's population increased, it was obvious that something had to be done to gain more land. Do you know what they did?"

The drains Inspector sat upright, and started launching into a description of land reclamation in Holland where land was reclaimed from the sea and dykes controlled the system.

Simon explained how an airport had been built on top of debris poured into the sea in Japan and Percy sat and fumed because *this was his story.*

117

"Anyway," Percy interrupted, "my ancestor had the amazing idea of turning all the big mountains upside down; this would put the pointy end at the bottom and leave more room in between them."

After a silence, the drains inspector said diplomatically, "Well, Percy, I can see a few problems with that one."

"Yes, yes, I know," said Percy, holding up his hands. "All the snow fell off and blocked the spaces again, but it was soon cleared away."

Buster, ever keen to learn and improve himself, asked, "So what happened, did they do it?"

"No, it was all stopped by big business as usual. They objected to all the souvenirs having to be scrapped and re-made, and the mountaineers were inconsolable. What was the point of climbing for all those hours just to walk across a flat plain and have a picnic?"

The road gang walked back to the depot in a dream, silently handed the face-mask to Marvin, and went off to compile reports of deeds worthy of re-telling by *their* ancestors.

Marvin sat alone at the bar in a room well away from the women.

Henry cleaned glasses nearby and prepared to listen. He could recognise the signs. This man had been sent out 'to give her some peace' and 'have a moment alone' probably garnished with 'do I rule every moment of *your* life?'

Marvin stared into his glass as if the instruction book of marriage was in there somewhere.

Henry moved closer and furrowed his brow. "Doreen all right, Marvin?" he asked, lighting the fuse.

Marvin clenched his fists, stretched his mouth wide and shook. "Doreeen!" he spat, "Doreeen! If I took her a bag of gold, it would be the wrong colour bag!" He threw the drink back and thumped his glass on the bar the way they did in westerns. "Fill 'er up!" he slurred.

Henry pulled a fresh pint pretending he had some control with the size of its head, and handed it over.

Marvin wrapped his hands around the glass as if the hops could soak straight through and save themselves a journey. Then he continued. "Find me a magic face mask, she said. Do I look like an adventurer? It will be a golden fleece next!"

"Didn't the mask work?" asked Henry, surprised.

Marvin glowered into the glass as if he had found the instruction book, but the page was missing. "I don't know," wailed Marvin. "I handed it over and she scrunched it up, screamed 'I send you for a face mask and you bring me a Nan-bread' and slapped it onto my forehead!" He continued, "I stormed out, I can tell you. As soon as she couldn't hear me I slammed the door too."

Henry had to admit that Marvin's forehead was looking remarkably smooth, but before he could comment, Marvin continued, "On top of all that I have to come up with a suitable motto for the Local Authority by the end of the week." His head dropped pathetically.

Of course Henry could simply not resist. "How about," he suggested, "never in the field of human conflict have so many been so confused by so few."

Cuthbert sat very still. Percy was beside him. He also sat very still. The women fussed around them. They were patted, fed, watered and, in Percy's case, dusted.

Cups of tea and plates of scones were laid reverently before them. It would have been the dream of most men, except for the curious fact that Arkle was blocking the door.

Cuthbert and Percy sat at the head of the long table and the women now ranged down both sides. Arkle stayed where she was, arms folded like a cigar store Indian.

Margery smiled.

Teeth rippled all the way around the table as the rest followed suit.

The two men exchanged looks. They were tempted to hold hands under the table. Percy whispered nervously, "When did you last see your father?"

Cuthbert began wracking his brains to answer. "Just after I accidentally shot him," he announced loudly.

The smiles faded and eyes flickered nervously.

Cuthbert turned to his friend and said, "No, I tell a lie! I saw him when I laid him out. I remember, because it was the only time we were in each other's company without him saying 'Not again, Cuthbert'."

Percy stared at his friend hoping this was a clever strategy to help them escape, but the eyes saw nothing but Cuthbert beaming back at him. Percy was trapped. He couldn't think of any good stories and he wasn't wearing his assault vest. With a resigned sigh, he turned to the women and asked, "What do you want?"

The women had gone. The unexpected bonus was that they had reclaimed all the curtains and fripperies.

The kitchen was back to being a sparse but homely bachelor cell.

Percy looked at Cuthbert and said, "So, you're the great white hope for the Valley then?"

Cuthbert replied, "Pardon?"

Percy watched him keenly, "You *were* listening, weren't you?"

Cuthbert sniffed. "Course not, you asked me a question and it brought back memories. I was miles away."

Percy explained matters to Cuthbert slowly, ending with, "And tomorrow some celebrity chef will come and make a film about your attempt to win the baking competition."

Cuthbert considered this. "Am I free tomorrow?"

"Yes," said Percy.

"How do you know?" asked Cuthbert.

"Because some celebrity chef is coming to film your attempt to win the baking competition."

Cuthbert stroked his chin. "That's a coincidence."

Arkle sat on a saddle, alone in her room. She had just heard the news.

Felicity Washbrook was coming to the Valley. Felicity had been an idol to Arkle for years, the way she seemed to address *only you* as she spoke to the camera and it was *you* personally being invited to join her in some exotic location for a meal.

Arkle had been known to ride into the nearest big town and stare at the TV screens in shop windows on certain nights when the programme was scheduled. Now she was coming to the Valley. She would taste *her* pastry! It was one of her dreams come true. Arkle began to relive one of Felicity's recent programmes where the mixture was particularly exotic and the chef had run her fingers around the bowl and sensuously licked them.

Arkle's hand was half way to her mouth when she thought better

120

of it; she had just wormed the horse.

Chapter Eighteen

Cuthbert awoke to the clanking of pans, the mutter of conversation and finally to a shrill scream. Snuggling into his covers, he smiled and waited for his mum to wake him for school. He used to fantasise that he had woken up in a castle and the knights were putting on armour and yelling for their horses.

Percy burst into his room and threw back the shutters. "They're here!" he yelled. "Up you get, Cuthbert."

Cuthbert muttered, "Coming mum, nearly dressed."

Percy whipped the sheet off, spinning Cuthbert to the floor. "Come on! They're setting up the equipment." He then disappeared like the rabbit in Alice in Wonderland.

Cuthbert shambled down to find his kitchen full of people, well, three extra people anyway. A man setting up microphones nodded to Cuthbert. Another man setting up a huge camera waved to him vaguely whilst holding a cable and scratching his head.

Percy sat cross-legged on the table staring in rapture at the voluptuous creature bashing the pans together. With a wave of his hand, he introduced his new love. "This is Felicity Washbrook."

Felicity clanged the pans together one last time and glared at Cuthbert. "Is this some kind of joke?" she shrilled. "Did those idiots at the agency set this up to get me back? Speak man."

Cuthbert slowly absorbed the vision in his kitchen. This woman's jumpers could give Belinda a run for her money. The jet black hair tumbled to her shoulders and the red lips tightened.

"Kitchener was the last person to use these, over an open fire!" she ranted.

The sound man muttered, "Kitchen-er, oh, very good." The gravy brown eyes swept over him, dismissed him as a necessary buffoon and focused on Cuthbert.

"Where is the chrome? My kitchens have chrome. *All* kitchens have chrome."

"Some even have electricity," muttered the sound man.

"What!" shrieked Felicity.

The man shrugged and waved his cable end dejectedly. Felicity headed for Cuthbert like the Santa Maria under full sail. "You don't

122

have electricity?"

Cuthbert shook his head proudly.

The woman gaped. "What am I going to cook on?"

A subdued hiss followed by a puff of smoke alerted her to the culinary monster by the wall. Felicity gasped and steadied herself against the table.

"Call my agent," she gasped to the sound man. "I don't *do* historical recreations; she knows that."

"She won't know it today," he smirked. "No signal."

Felicity looked at Cuthbert; then she looked at Percy. "And is this your little helper?" she asked acidly.

Batteries had been fitted to the cameras and the microphones, and Felicity was positioned to her best advantage.

"Camera check!" called the cameraman.

Felicity smiled at the lens. Her face softened and her lips pursed seductively.

"Sound check!" called the sound man.

Felicity slowly licked her lips and purred for posterity. Gone was the strident critic of country cooking and all those who lived near it. She beamed into the camera ready to charm her way into a million households.

Cuthbert stood to one side and tried to spot who she was talking to and Percy stood the other side gazing up adoringly at her. "This is Cuthbert," she purred, lowering her head coquettishly so that the eyebrow flutter would be noticed. "He is the surprise entrant for this year's Baking Jamboree which will be shown nationwide very soon." Glancing down at Percy as if something furry had just run across her foot she added, "And this is his helper Posey."

Both the sound man and cameraman declared themselves happy and everyone relaxed. Off-camera Felicity resurfaced immediately as she carped about absolutely everything.

Percy came out of his reverie and dashed outside to pick some flowers for Felicity. Cables snaked across the ground to a large van that stood with its sliding door open. The two main cables were unplugged and it was obvious they should be fitted together.

Percy tutted about 'sloppy workmanship' and plugged them in. Looking inside the van he realised he had probably just saved the day and he would be Felicity's hero. The van was full of flickering screens and consoles.

Percy sat at one of them and pretended to play the organ. Every time he neared the right hand side of the console his fingers strayed towards a button with a hinged cover over it. *Why put a cover over a button?* wondered Percy. Looking around, he flipped the cover up and pressed the button. Apart from a faint whirring noise the result was disappointing, so he put the cover back down.

Above the van a thirty foot tall telescopic aerial deployed and began beaming back a live transmission.

Returning with a bunch of hogweed from near the stile, Percy simpered over to Felicity and presented them to her.

Felicity was again practising a piece 'to camera' and she took the bundle from him and rapidly chopped them into a garnish. Turning to the cooking range she hefted a huge iron frying pan and swung it in a ponderous arc towards the table, catching Percy on the side of the head as she did so. Percy reeled sideways and clutched the table just as Felicity put the red hot pan on his fingers.

Cuthbert watched in fascination as Percy leapt about, seemingly welded to the table.

The soundman called, "Cut!" and Felicity wielded a cleaver.

Percy fainted. As her crew tried to revive Percy, Felicity ranted at them all. She blamed her 'dumb agent', her 'dumb film crew' and the 'dumb public' for having nothing better to do than watch someone else break eggs.

Cuthbert was fascinated by the blinking light on the camera and practised his smile in the reflection of the lens.

Felicity turned on *him*. Apparently he lived in a misbegotten cow shed with a scarecrow named Posey and didn't have the social graces of a skunk.

"Even those fools who commission the programme should have seen that 'Joe Public and Josephine Housewife' wouldn't fall for a contrived story like this one."

The sound man had been out to the van for a bottle of water for Percy, and he returned ashen-faced. "Er, Felicity," he began.

Felicity stopped in mid rant, assuming it was another 'piece to camera' and instantly switched to her T.V. persona smoothly, asking Cuthbert whether "*she* could live in such a gloriously rural spot such as this wonderful Valley?"

Cuthbert said innocently she certainly had something the Valley women didn't possess.

Felicity asked demurely, "What might that be, Cuthbert?" accompanied by flapping eyelashes.

Cuthbert, thinking of the pastry facemasks, replied, "Wrinkles!"

Felicity demonstrated her acting skills with an imitation of a landed cod. "Did you hear that?" she screamed at the sound man. "Could he have said anything worse to me than that?"

"Well," replied the sound man, "he could have said that we've been going out live for twenty minutes."

Cuthbert and Percy watched the van screech down the farm lane trailing cables behind it. The antennae on top strummed the telephone wires as it passed and the crows perched on them did a 'Mexican wave' in farewell.

The last straw seemed to be just as Felicity was leaving. A huge woman had thrown herself forward booming, "Felicity, Felicity. How was my pastry?" The celebrity chef fled for the van with the fan in hot pursuit and the smell of horse in her nostrils. Arkle gave up and came back into the kitchen. "Why didn't she try my pastry?" she asked menacingly.

Cuthbert still had traces of adrenalin in his sluggish system and risked, "Yours? I thought it was *our* pastry?"

Arkle's body turned towards him as if she was preparing to fire a broadside.

Cuthbert stammered, "At least that's what Percy thought anyway."

Percy saw the shadow fall across him and shivered.

"Where is my pastry?" she asked like the hiss of a cobra.

Percy silently pointed to a really good likeness of Beethoven on the table.

Again the hiss. "Who did this?"

Percy stammered, "M-m-me."

Another hiss. "Who is it?"

"B-B-Beethoven," he managed.

Arkle stepped forward and hammered her fist straight down onto the top of the sculptures head. Now it looked like a Halloween pumpkin. Then she punched it straight in the face leaving her hand deep inside it. With a twist and a wrench she pulled the middle out, turned it round and stuck it back on upside down. "Now it's a self-portrait," she declared and left.

Chapter Nineteen

The bar at the Mandrake arms was buzzing. "Now that's what I call 'Reality TV'," said Marjorie. "It was just like being in the room when an aunt has a nervous breakdown. Or so I imagine," she added hastily.

Elspeth shook her head. "Poor Felicity. Fancy sending her to meet those two on their home turf- frightening."

Avril exclaimed, "I was watching the news and they suddenly broke into it with a live transmission."

Henry shook his head sadly. "I had years in front of the cameras. You have to think on your feet. 'Dead air' when everyone dries up is bad enough, but 'Live air' is terrifying. She insulted everyone, she'll never work again, I'm afraid."

The bar went silent. Ronald spoke up. "It's her own fault. Reality TV," he scoffed. "Fancy coming into the Valley and expecting to find reality!"

Everyone nodded sombrely.

Percy turned back into the room and shouted at Cuthbert. "There's a man at the door with a bill!"

"Are you sure it's not a duck with a hat on?" answered Cuthbert automatically.

Percy sighed. Cuthbert didn't know many jokes, but when he learnt one he really wore it out. "Come in," he said stepping out of the way.

Two men entered and looked around curiously. One held an itemised list in his hand. Trying to tear his eyes away from Percy sculpting a reclining nude with Beethoven's hairstyle out of pastry, he addressed Cuthbert. "We've come to collect your cooker and take it to the regional finals."

Cuthbert and Percy exchanged looks. "Why would you do that?" asked Cuthbert.

The man stared at him. "That's what all the competitors demand. They use their own cooker and implements, but everything is watched by the judges on the day."

Cuthbert scratched his chin. "Well, if you can shift it you can take

127

it."

Percy added, "And if no-one claims it in six months' time, it's yours."

The two men accepted the challenge and assembled an array of tools on the floor.

Cuthbert took a ring-side seat across the table from them.

Percy joined him after dragging his reclining nude Beethoven out of the way. One of the men slid a long iron bar under the cooking range and lifted it. The other man lay down and shone a torch underneath. "Can't see any bolts. It's not fastened down."

The other man lowered it. "Right then we'll whip that stove-pipe off it and lever it out this way" he said.

The other man grabbed the metal chimney and wrenched it from side to side to loosen it.

One of the oven doors crept open. "Oh, oh!" said Percy.

Cuthbert asked, "Won't it be too hot to handle?"

A voice replied, "Not after we've dragged it out and turned a hosepipe on it … aaaaaarghhh!"

The flame could have burnt the table or set fire to the room. It did neither. With surgical precision, it burnt through both straps on the man's bib and brace overalls and removed his side-burns. The man stood there in a puddle of clothing showing off his polka-dot shorts and with scorch marks on each cheek.

"Is that why they call them side-burns then?" asked Percy.

"Must be," said Cuthbert.

The second man had succeeded in loosening the top of the chimney and the range coughed soot right in his face. 'Al Jolson' looked at 'Polka-dot' and they both reached for the biggest hammer in the pile.

The cooking range fought back. Red hot cinders rolled across the floor. Jets of flame lanced in all directions as doors and lids opened and closed in a searing symphony. Tools clonked, smoke belched and curses flew.

'Al Jolson' lost one leg of his jeans and his moustache.

'Polka-dot' swung the hammer, but was disorientated by a sudden cloud of smoke and he flattened his colleague's steel toe-cap into the floor. This went on for an hour and a half; eventually the two men stood back, panting with exertion. The cooking range panted right back at them.

'Polka-dot' turned to Cuthbert and said, "I'm sorry, mate. This one doesn't seem to be coming with us."

Cuthbert looked resigned, but Percy said, "It's all right, mate, we're only entered in the salad section."

Chapter Twenty

This time the bar of the Mandrake Arms really was full, even Percy and Cuthbert were there.

Henry chewed his lip as he re-read the rules. "The whole point of the competition is for people to use their own cooker and appliances," he said. "If that is the cooker which produced the pastry that is the cooker which should compete, I'm afraid."

Cuthbert sank in his chair. All he ever wanted from life was to be left alone in case he ever found a hobby to occupy his time. Why was he always the focus for potential disaster? He found himself imagining the scene if the cooking range really had to be taken across the country. He imagined it chuffing away gently on the back of a huge wagon pulled by Percy's tractor. It would be like taking a favourite fat aunt to the seaside- everybody loves her but you hope no-one sees you together.

Margery was incensed. "It's the least you could do, Cuthbert. You represent the Valley and all our combined cooking skills. Would it have killed you to have knocked a wall down and dragged the wretched thing out?" She paused for breath and hurtled on. "If it was *my* cooker, *I* would have moved heaven and earth for the Valley!"

"*Actually*!" said a voice.

Everyone automatically looked at Avril, but it was Arkle who spoke. "I made the pastry on *your* cooker. The boys just finished it off on theirs."

All eyes swivelled towards Margery. "Oh!" she said.

Cuthbert was pacing up and down and the cooking range watched him warily.

Percy started to feel queasy; it was like being at a tennis match. "Sit, Cuthbert," he said, "they will be here in a minute."

The committee from the competition were due to visit to resolve the problem of the cooking range.

Percy went to the window and said, "Here we go, two people coming to the door, one of them is 'Polka-dot shorts' and the other is a woman with a clip-board."

The two visitors entered the kitchen and 'Polka-dot' explained the problem while standing well away from the offending article. The woman made notes and studied the cooking range from every angle. Tapping a pencil against perfect teeth, she said, "I'm sorry, but the rules state that the entry must be prepared under the eyes of the judges with the competitor's own appliance."

Margery appeared between Cuthbert and Percy and a panel in the wall slid shut behind her. Trying to make amends and show solidarity she grabbed one each of Cuthbert and Percy's hands and gave them a squeeze.

Cuthbert hadn't been paying attention and he thought it was Percy. Blushing crimson, he asked, "Is there nothing we can do?"

The woman saw his change of colour and said, "Oh dear, you're not having a heart attack, are you?"

Margery gave another squeeze and Cuthbert spluttered, "I may well be!"

The woman desperately tried to mollify him. "I really don't think this old thing would have survived the journey anyway," and gave a contemptuous wave of her hand.

The double oven doors slammed open and a soft blue flame engulfed her for a split second. As the doors slowly closed again with a mocking creak, the woman watched her clip-board wilt before her and drip onto the floor just before her mascara stuck her eye lashes together and she had to be led away.

As the car drove away Cuthbert felt another squeeze and a peck on his cheek. "That went rather well," purred a voice in his ear. Cuthbert trembled.

"I suppose it did really," said Percy from across the room. Cuthbert turned sharply, saw Margery and nearly had the heart attack that he had nearly had before.

Margery addressed the crowded bar once more. "Honour is saved, everyone. After special consideration, in special circumstances Cuthbert has been allowed to provide the centre-piece for the celebration feast at the end of the competition. It will be seen by all and will receive a special prize of its own." The Valley inhabitants responded with a polite round of applause.

Cuthbert and Percy waited in the other room ready for their grand entrance. They were starting to fidget.

"And now, the piece de resistance! Put your hands together for La chef surprise!"

The crowd in the bar craned around and realised what a limited joint the neck was, when Margery gave up and yelled, *"Cuthbert! Get out here!"*

Cuthbert suddenly appeared in the room as if someone had kicked him.

Ronald was close behind.

Margery put her hands over her eyes in despair. "*With* the centrepiece Cuthbert!" she wailed.

Cuthbert went back in, but Percy was sulking. After all his hard work, Cuthbert went out first and therefore took all the credit. Cuthbert pleaded with him before Margery came to get them. "What can I do to cheer you up?" he asked.

Percy squeezed his hand, puckered up and said, "Gizza kiss!"

Cuthbert and Percy staggered into the room with a huge round platter covered in a cloth. "Is that one of Cuthbert's curtains?" asked Elspeth.

Margery was racking up the suspense by intoning, "This is a complete surprise to us all; only Cuthbert and Percy know the answer to this mystery."

"That's a first," contributed Ronald.

The huge centre-piece was thumped down onto an equally large round table and Percy whipped away the cloth to be greeted by ... silence.

It was round, it had a dip in the middle and there were seemingly random shapes scattered around a winding path caused by Cuthbert dragging his finger across the pastry.

The men were watching both the women and the exits at the same time and the women were watching each other.

Arkle broke the silence with, "Huh, even *my* pastry doesn't sink in the middle."

"*It's the Valley!*" spluttered Cuthbert. "Look, there's the road and these are all the houses, the pub and the church."

The women leaned in closer and the men exhaled.

Margery slapped Percy's hand as he tried to eat the Post Office and the whole atmosphere relaxed until Avril asked, "Is that an earthquake then?"

Joe-Crow popped his black head and yellow beak through the crust like something from a science fiction film.

The crowd gasped and stepped back. The rest of the crows were fed up too and the middle of the landscape exploded into flapping wings and scattered crumbs. It was chaos.

The crowd stampeded in all directions and the crows stampeded above them.

Elspeth grabbed for a dustpan and brush. "Oh, look at all the mess, all the feathers. It will take ages to clean it up; there must be at least four and twenty of the blooming things!"

~ The End ~

About the Author

Patrick Barrett is a sixty year old ex-miner from Mansfield in Nottinghamshire. He is married to Paula and between them, they have several children. 'Shakespeare's Cuthbert' was his first book, though he has been writing comedy for several years.

His aims as a writer are 'to be successful and make people laugh by providing them with an escape from the harshness of real life'.

His other abiding interest is in antiques.

www.ingramcontent.com/pod-product-compliance
Lightning Source LLC
Chambersburg PA
CBHW050901180626
46814CB00007B/2827